Puffin Books

the Quay

The story opens in the living-room of the
Four Masters' Bookshop on Ormond Quay
in Dublin, on an autumn evening. The
bookseller Eugene O'Clery, his wife Eilis,
his schoolboy son Patrick, his nine-year-old
daughter Bridgie, with her beloved cat Mog
and her rag-doll Migeen, together with the
O'Clerys' faithful old servant, the Widow
Flanagan, are seated at high tea. They are
reading books propped against milk jugs
(the room is full of books) or staring at the
traffic by the Liffey and at the people
hunched against the cold east wind blowing
in from Dublin Bay.

Into this setting comes Shane Madden, a
runaway orphan searching for his dashing
but unreliable hero, Uncle Tim. How Shane
finds work in the bookshop in Dublin and
succeeds in his quest is the theme of this
charming and vivid story which will be
enjoyed by boys and girls of ten and over.

Patricia Lynch

The Bookshop
on the Quay

With illustrations by Peggy Fortnum

Puffin Books

Puffin Books: a Division of Penguin Books Ltd,
Harmondsworth, Middlesex, England
Penguin Books Australia Ltd, Ringwood,
Victoria, Australia
Penguin Books Canada Ltd,
41 Steelcase Road West, Markham, Ontario,
Canada
Penguin Books (N.Z.) Ltd,
182–190 Wairau Road, Auckland 10,
New Zealand

First published by Dent 1956
Published in Puffin Books 1964
Reprinted 1968, 1974
Copyright © Patricia Lynch, 1956

Made and printed in Great Britain by
Richard Clay (The Chaucer Press) Ltd,
Bungay, Suffolk
Set in Monotype Fournier

Contents

To Sioban

1. Stop Thief!

The O'Clerys were having tea in the big, comfortable room behind the bookshop.

Mr O'Clery sat facing the window overlooking the lane leading up from the Liffey. His grey hair stood on end and his eyes sparkled as he sipped the hot strong tea. Mrs O'Clery and Patrick, their son, were opposite, side by side. Bridgie, who was only nine, perched on the edge of the big wooden armchair, the cat, Mog, stretched beside her. She could see through the archway into the shop and, where the window was clear, to Ormond Quay.

Even now, when a big open book was standing against the glass, Bridgie could see the double-decker buses from the country hurtling past, the funnel of a Guinness barge puffing down the river towards O'Connell Bridge, swans rising on their great wings, sea-gulls soaring into the blue sky and turning silver in the pale evening sunshine. Further along there were men leaning on the river wall, their shoulders hunched against the cold wind blowing in from Dublin Bay.

'Someone should tell me a story about it all,' murmured Bridgie.

Without noticing, she saw the fair, grey-eyed boy who stood outside, reading the big open book in the window.

The shop had shelves from the floor to the ceiling, all crowded with books. There were loaded tables on each side and down the centre. In the living-room books were stacked in corners, on the window-sill, and upstairs the attic doors couldn't be closed because bundles of books were always being stowed there.

Mr O'Clery had a book propped against the milk jug. Two others were poked in the sides of his armchair, a very thick volume was at the back, pushing him forward. Every time he put down his cup he reached back and felt the binding, smiling with pleasure at the rich softness of the leather.

Mrs O'Clery, though she always said reading at table was the worst of bad manners, drank her tea with a paper-covered book tucked under the edge of her plate. Patrick, who was twelve, had a talent for drawing, and he studied a page of strange letters he had copied from an old book.

Bridgie thought it most unfair that her father objected to her bringing her doll to meals. Migeen was a rag doll, made by the Widow Flanagan and, though most people thought it ugly, Bridgie loved Migeen almost as much as Mog the cat.

'Even if I am nine,' she thought, 'a rag doll isn't like an ordinary doll, just a toy. It's almost a person!'

Then Bridgie really saw the boy outside the window – a boy with fair, rumpled hair, a dirty face, and mournful grey eyes. He gazed at the *Gulliver's Travels* displayed there as if he were meeting a friend. Craning her neck, Bridgie saw that his coat was muddy and wrinkled, and he carried an untidy bundle under his arm.

'The poor boy!' she said to Mog. 'He's lost!'

As she spoke, the boy looked over the book, across the shop, and Bridgie felt he was staring at the piece of kipper on its way to her mouth.

'He's hungry!' she said aloud, laying down the loaded fork.

Only Mog heard her and he took advantage of Bridgie's interest in the strange boy to raise a greedy paw, snatch the tail of the kipper, and leap to the floor.

'Robber!' exclaimed Bridgie.

She didn't want any-
one to know Mog stole.
Not even Mrs Flanagan,
who lived with the
O'Clerys and did the
cooking and cleaning,
was sure about Mog's
honesty. The cat was
supposed to have his
food in the kitchen but
Bridgie liked his warmth

and softness, and he obligingly ate the bits she didn't want.

The little girl sat with her elbows on each side of the plate,
gripping her cup with both hands. Her silky black hair fell
over her clear blue eyes but she saw everything which happened outside as well as inside. She pretended not to see the
boy. He might go away if he caught her looking and she
wondered who he was and where he had come from.

'Hate kippers!' grumbled Mr O'Clery. 'Too many bones!'

'And when I gave ye boneless kippers last Wednesday, ye
gave out and hadn't a good word to say for them!' cried the
Widow Flanagan, from the dark, tiny kitchen. 'And when it's
good Dublin Bay herrings I put before ye and they done to a
turn, ye don't like herrings! What does yer lordship like?'

'I do like kippers!' protested Mr O'Clery, pushing away
his empty plate, 'but not boneless kippers, tasteless, dried-up,
unnatural things, while these have more than their rightful
share of bones!'

'Mog likes kipper bones and I like the lovely smell!' murmured Bridgie.

Mog gave a faint miaow of agreement. He knew he
wouldn't have long to wait for the rest of the kipper now that
talking had commenced.

Patrick put down his cup and gazed earnestly at his father.
'There was a man in today,' he said, 'while you were out.

He left a message. I promised to tell you the moment you came in but I forgot. He has a collection of books he wants to sell at once. He's going to England and he lives in Monkstown.'

'Good lad!' said Mrs O'Clery, pouring him another cup of tea and pushing over the dish of toasted barm brack.

'Wants to sell quickly!' exclaimed Mr O'Clery. 'And the bicycle has both tyres flat!'

'I'll mend them for you the moment I've finished tea!' said Patrick.

'And destroy them altogether!' chuckled his father. 'I know your mending!'

'Eugene! You can't expect Patrick to be good at everything!' said the bookseller's wife. 'Bridgie, what are you staring at?'

'The boy!' explained Bridgie. 'He's been there reading the book in the window for hours and hours and hours!'

The others turned and stared too.

'I remember noticing him when I poured out the tea!' said Mrs O'Clery.

'He's certainly interested in that *Gulliver's Travels*,' chuckled Mr O'Clery. 'I knew it would draw customers.'

'He wouldn't have the money to buy a book!' declared Patrick. 'He's just reading all he can for nothing!'

'He's tired, and he wants a kipper too!' sighed Bridgie, shaking her head as she glanced regretfully at the fish bones on her plate.

'He can have my tea. I've only drunk half a cup and there's heaps of barm brack left,' she reflected.

She put down the plate for Mog and bent over the cat, listening to the talk going on around the table.

'That boy has certainly been there a long time!' declared Mr O'Clery. 'He must be learning those two pages by heart. Isn't it grand to see such interest, Eilis?'

'I wonder!' said his wife. 'I'm afraid he's in trouble. He's only a young lad and he looks terribly tired. Maybe I should speak to him!'

She looked from the boy at the window to her own children, thankful they were safe and cared for.

'Suppose it was Patrick?' she thought.

They sat watching the boy. He shivered and hunched his shoulders against the cold east wind coming in from the bay. His hands rested on the magazines and cheap books lying on the ledge outside.

'He looks frightened and he's not much more than a child,' murmured Mrs O'Clery.

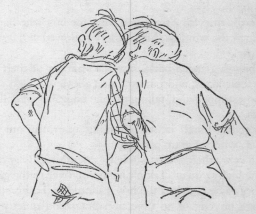

Suddenly two ragged boys came running along the quay, one in the gutter, the other on the kerb. They stopped and began pushing one another. They whispered, then leaped across the pavement, thrusting the young reader away.

As he staggered, dropping his bundle, each ragamuffin grabbed an armful of books and magazines and ran round the side of the shop, up the lane.

At once the other boy raced after them, while the book-seller jumped up, sending a book flying to the floor and up-setting the jug of milk. He rushed through the shop and out to the pavement, bumping against the tables as he went and scattering books on the floor.

Patrick went after him, while Bridgie stood jumping up and down in the doorway.

'What's the commotion?' asked the Widow Flanagan, pulling her shawl over her head as she came from the kitchen.

'Thieves!' sighed Mrs O'Clery. 'We must stop having books outside the shop. It's a temptation, though it does bring customers.'

'If the master will leave reading outside the shop, unprotected, what else can he expect?' cried the widow. 'He should have a shop boy!'

On ran the thieves! After them went the boy who had been looking in at the window. Mr O'Clery followed and last of all came Patrick.

The thieves glanced back, saw the stranger at their heels, dropped their loads, and ran up a side alley.

The boy stopped and, falling on one knee, began collecting the books.

'They're not hurt!' he said, holding an armful out to the bookseller, who came up panting.

'You'll carry them back yourself!' cried Mr O'Clery. 'And think how lucky you are I don't hand you over to the gardai!'

Wrathfully he clutched the boy's shoulder. To his surprise the strange boy made no objection but stood quietly while Patrick, who had caught up with them, gathered together the rest of the books.

'I didn't take them!' declared the boy. 'You know I didn't!'

'I saw you!' protested Mr O'Clery. 'You should be ashamed, stealing a man's books before his eyes!'

'I don't think he did, dadda!' said Patrick. 'It was the other boys. He ran after them!'

'He was with them!' persisted his father.

'I was not!' said the boy.

His eyes flashed. His face was red with indignation.

They reached the shop and Mrs Flanagan clapped her hands.

'Isn't it well ye caught one of them,' she cried. 'Make him tell ye the names of the others. Let Patrick ring up the gardai and have the young ruffian taken off to prison!'

'No!' exclaimed Bridgie.

'I'm sure he isn't a thief!' declared Patrick. 'Wasn't he looking in the window long before the others came up?'

'That's true,' agreed Mr O'Clery. 'I could have made a mistake.'

The boy put the books back on the ledge and arranged them as they were before. Then he stepped away and looked defiantly at the little group in the doorway.

'Can I go?' he asked.

The bookseller nodded. He was feeling ashamed.

Bridgie clutched the boy's hand.

'Let the strange boy have tea with us!' she said. 'He's tired and hungry, and he didn't take the books. He didn't!'

Mrs O'Clery, who had come out from the shop, stared thoughtfully at her daughter.

'Bridgie's right! We could all do with another cup of tea.'

She turned to the boy.

'If you're not expected home,' she said.

He took his hand away from Bridgie's hot clasp.

'I'll not stay where I've been called a thief!' he declared proudly.

Mr O'Clery shrugged his shoulders but his wife saw the weary droop of the boy's whole body.

'Don't be foolish,' she urged. 'It was a mistake! We're all very sorry!'

The boy could see the comfortable room behind the shop. He looked at the friendly anxious faces around him and, smiling down at Bridgie's thin face with its big intent blue eyes, he nodded.

'I'll be very thankful, ma'am,' he said. 'No one's expecting me!'

'The kettle's on the boil!' called the Widow Flanagan over her shoulder as she went off. 'And there's the bit of cold bacon!'

2. Shane Tells His Story

Mog, the cat, was in the kitchen clearing up the fishy plates, so there was room for the boy to sit beside Bridgie on the edge of the old wooden arm-chair.

'What is your name?' asked Mrs O'Clery, as she poured the fresh pot of tea.

'Shane Madden, ma'am!' the boy told her, trying not to take too big a mouthful of cold bacon.

'And where do you come from?' the bookseller wanted to know. 'You're no Dublin boy.'

'Two miles from Ballylicky, near the Cork road,' replied Shane slowly, frowning at Mr O'Clery over the steaming cup. He always hated being questioned.

It had been the tantalizing smell of kipper which had kept him at the shop window long after he had grown weary of the two pages of *Gulliver's Travels*.

Mrs O'Clery put down the teapot on the white table-cloth, forgetting the empty saucer waiting there.

'I knew you were no city boy!' she said.

The boy dropped his knife and fork and stood up. Bridgie tugged him down again.

'Don't answer if you don't want to,' said the bookseller kindly. 'We'll ask no more questions. Make a good tea. You're very welcome!'

He longed to prop up his book again but the milk jug, now refilled, was in front of the visitor and out of reach. Mrs

O'Clery fidgeted with a ball of wool. She was too troubled about the stranger to go on working. Patrick had forgotten him and was studying his drawings. Bridgie was content. She waited patiently, sure that Shane Madden had a story and would tell it.

'I'm looking for me uncle, Uncle Tim!' said the boy suddenly.

He went on drinking tea and eating the bacon slowly to taste every delicious bite, while the four sat watching.

When even Bridgie began to fear they had heard the last of Uncle Tim, the boy looked up with troubled eyes.

'I can't find him,' he said. 'I'm terrified I'll never see him again!'

'Keep on eating,' said Mrs O'Clery. 'When you've finished you can tell as much or as little as you like. We might be able to help you.'

Shane ate every bit of bacon on his plate and all the bread and butter and barm brack before him. He drank three cups of tea.

'You look a different boy,' the bookseller's wife told him, her serious face softening as she looked at him.

He couldn't help smiling back. He made up his mind. These people weren't inquisitive strangers. They were friends.

'Maybe I should begin at the beginning,' he said. 'There was always me and Uncle Tim. When me mother died, he had to give up the farm and he took me to Uncle Joseph's. I was that scared I was howling me eyes out and I could hardly walk. Of course I was only six then. It was a long time ago but Uncle Tim often told me about it. Aunt Maureen was alone in the house. She's Uncle Tim's sister. He said if Uncle Joseph had been there I'd have had something to howl about. She made up for everything!'

'Didn't your Uncle Joseph want you?' asked Mrs O'Clery sympathetically.

The boy shook his head.

'He didn't want me. He didn't even want Uncle Tim. If it hadn't been for Aunt Maureen we wouldn't have stayed the night. Me uncle said she'd give you her last crust and thank you for taking it.'

Shane sat silent, gazing into the darkened shop. The world outside was dim and filled with shadows but he was thinking of his aunt and the ugly little farmhouse, miles away in County Cork.

'Tell us some more!' whispered Bridgie.

The boy smiled at her and went on.

'Uncle Tim did all the work on the farm but Uncle Joseph always found fault. Then Uncle Tim became a drover. He could do anything he wished with animals and he was the best drover between Cork and Limerick. He paid Uncle Joseph for keeping him and me, and he always brought presents for us all. There was Des and Maggie and Jer and young Babs. He brought something for every one of us each time he went away.'

Shane's hands, lying on the table before him, were clenched. Bridgie squeezed closer to him.

'I like your Uncle Tim!' she said.

'Uncle Tim was only waiting for me to leave school. The day I was fourteen he said we'd go off together. He had to do a big job, take a herd of bullocks and some sheep and cows to the Fair at Ballybricken. He'd have a pocket full of money. Then we'd make plans, he said.'

'The day before,' and Shane spoke so softly they could scarcely hear him, 'Uncle Tim took me to Cork on the bus. We had our dinner in a grand eating-house near Patrick's

Bridge, and when he'd bought the presents for the others, we had tea there too. He bought a pair of gloves to wear on Sunday for Aunt Maureen, a tin of bacca for Uncle Joseph, a doll for Maggie, a doll's house for Babs, soldiers for Des, and building blocks for Jer.'

'I do like Uncle Tim,' murmured Bridgie.

'What did he buy you?' asked Patrick.

Shane looked at him proudly.

'He told me to choose. He said I was his bold comrade, so I wanted to choose something better than a toy. We came to a bookshop. The window was packed with old books but in the middle was one like the book in your window. Its name is *Gulliver's Travels* and it is written by someone called Dean Swift.'

'He came to Dublin too!' murmured Mr O'Clery, as he went softly from the room to shut the door of the shop.

He stood for a moment looking out on the deserted wind-swept quays with O'Connell Bridge in the distance – a blaze of light.

As he came back he switched on the lights, for they could scarcely see one another.

Shane didn't notice. He was back in Cork with Uncle Tim.

'I could listen to talk about Uncle Tim and *Gulliver's Travels* all night!' declared Mrs O'Clery. 'But there's to-morrow and I must know where this lad is spending the night!'

Shane blinked. He had forgotten where he was.

'I don't know!' he said.

Patrick looked at his mother.

'Shane can sleep with me, if he will,' he said. 'There's heaps of room!'

Mr and Mrs O'Clery studied one another's eyes. They both nodded, looking as relieved as they felt. Patrick stood up and walked to the foot of the stairs which rose into darkness at the back of the shop. He jerked his thumb towards it.

'Come along, Shane Madden!'

He led the way. Shane picked up his bundle and followed.

'Time you were in bed, young madam!' Mrs O'Clery told her daughter.

Bridgie put Mog under her arm.

'*Gulliver's Travels?*' she asked, her head on one side.

The bookseller looked at his wife. They had a way of consulting one another silently.

'Why not?' she said, laughing. 'Bridgie won't understand half of it, but does it matter?'

Mr O'Clery, without bothering to switch on the light, felt his way to the big book in the window. It was heavy and he hesitated as Bridgie, who had followed him, dropped the cat and held out her arms.

'I'm not too sure it's good for you to be reading in bed!' he muttered.

'Isn't bed the best place for reading?' she asked in amazement.

It was difficult for her to climb the steep steps with the big book under her arm and the cat stepping close beside her. Half-way up she paused and looked back. Her father and mother were watching her.

'Bless you!' said Mrs O'Clery.

'Happy dreams!' called Mr O'Clery. 'Even if she doesn't read a page, Dean Swift should feel flattered!' he added, laughing.

The window of Bridgie's room was still open in spite of the cold. She laid the book on the window-seat beside her rag doll.

'Too heavy!' she grumbled. 'And the pictures are ugly. Patrick should read that book and tell me the story.'

The moon was rising over the spire and tower of St Patrick's and Christ Church on the far side of the Liffey.

Her father had told the children of that strange man, Dean Swift, who had lived there long ago. Below, on the dark waters of the river, the swans drifted asleep, their wings folded. Mog, purring beside her, leapt to the sill below and vanished into Patrick's room.

Bridgie could hear the boys' astonished laughter.

'That's a lovely cat!' said Shane. 'So small and such a bushy tail!'

He snapped his fingers. Mog stood on his hind legs and trotted across the floor.

'How did you know Mog could do that?' demanded Patrick, a trifle resentful. 'Twas I taught him!'

'Uncle Tim made the cat at home do all kinds of tricks!' said Shane. 'Can yours turn somersaults?'

Patrick shook his head.

'I'll teach Mog if you like,' offered Shane. 'Here, puss!'

Mog stalked over, purring, sat before the boys, and gazed reflectively at his tail curled elegantly about his front paws.

Shane bent down, lifted the cat, and rolled him gently across the floor. Suddenly Mog sprang away, leaped to the window sill, and went off into the night.

'You can't hurry Mog!' said Patrick cheerfully. 'He takes his own time!'

A wooden bed, with low stout posts at the corners, crowded the little room. A hurley stick leaned in one corner, football boots were upside-down in another. An enamel wash-basin was perched on an orange-box with soap and a flannel. Patrick's winter coat and Sunday suit swung from hooks at the back of the door.

The boys hung their clothes on the bedposts. While Patrick lay on his back, hands clasped behind his head, Shane unrolled his bundle, taking out the crumpled pyjamas, the comb and toothbrush he had packed before leaving the farm.

'I wonder where your Uncle Tim is now,' said Patrick, reaching up to switch off the light, while Shane sat beside him, arms encircling his knees, his head resting on them.

'I wanted him to take me with him to Ballybricken Fair!' muttered Shane. 'Why didn't he take me?'

3. Tim Madden

Shane, his eyes half-closed, was no longer in the room looking out over the Liffey. He was back in his Uncle Joseph's farmhouse, with the stained walls and the low slate roof, back with Uncle Tim in the narrow lean-to they had shared.

Red-headed Tim Madden lay on his back on the stretcher bed and Shane, his nephew, sat cross-legged on the floor, listening and watching.

'Ye needn't think I'm settled for the rest of me life on this back of beyond farm, young Shane!' declared Tim. 'The day ye leave school we're up and off with us!'

Shane hugged the book he had been reading and gazed at his uncle in delighted bewilderment.

'Only another three months!' he gasped.

Tim Madden raised himself on his elbows.

'Sure, ye can't be that old!' he cried. 'And what about me? Am I nearly twenty-five already? Pon me word, we'll have to stir ourselves! And I thinking it was only last year I brought ye here, that scared, ye were howling yer eyes out! Lucky Maureen was alone in the house. If Joseph had been here ye'd have had something to howl about!'

'Didn't he want me?' asked Shane mournfully, though indeed he knew the answer.

Tim laughed.

'He didn't want ye and he didn't want me, the old curmudgeon, though well he knew he was getting a good worker for nothing. If it wasn't for Maureen I wouldn't have stayed the night!'

Shane nodded. Aunt Maureen almost made up for Uncle Joseph. But he'd never forget that first night!

'There's only the two of us left!' said Uncle Tim. 'If himself will let us stay, I'll work the skin off me hands. Ye know I'm not afeard of work!'

'I know that well, Tim!' said Maureen. 'I'll love to have you. Only Joe isn't very sociable and the farm is a poor small class of a place!'

With her quick friendly smile and the toss of her head that sent her soft, reddish brown hair falling about her face, she seemed lovely to the small frightened boy.

'I was never a farm worker!' Tim told her. 'I'll find a job and bring in money to pay for the boy and meself. Ye'll be at no loss through me!'

Joseph Keating gave the young man and the boy a grudging welcome. Maureen was different. She missed the gay life at home, near Cork City. She was always telling the children of its wonderful shops and the marvellous times she and her brother Tim had when they were young.

Tim soon found work taking cattle to the market. He had a way with animals and each week he was busier. Even Joseph was glad of his help and Shane tried to be useful. Yet it was hard for the older man not to find fault.

'What will we do when the lad leaves school?' Joseph often asked. 'I've two boys of me own. I have to think of them!'

'No need to vex yourself about Shane!' declared Maureen. 'Tim will see to him.'

'When I come back from Waterford we'll make our plans,' Tim told the boy. 'I'll not stay a drover till I'm too old and weak to walk behind a cow!'

'Couldn't you take me with you to Waterford?' pleaded Shane.

His uncle looked doubtful.

'No, lad! No mitching! Ye're getting little enough education as it is and ye so fond of books. Finish with the school in style, so that even Joseph can't say a word against ye. This job is the best I've ever had and this time I won't waste the money. I'll keep enough to pay our fares to Dublin. Ye'll like Dublin!'

'I'd love it!' declared Shane.

'I'll surely find friends at the Cattle Market who'll put me in the way of work. Ye can help, and before we're much older we'll be on our travels. After Dublin then on to Liverpool. Ye've never been on a boat, a real boat. It's grand!'

'I saw great ships and we in Cork!' the boy reminded Tim.

'Then there's Ameriky,' said the young man dreamily. 'That's the country for a clever hard-working chap. There'd be respect for a good drover who was a champion into the bargain. Only it costs a mint of money to get there unless they'd let us work our passage.'

'I don't care where I go if I'm with you!' cried the boy.

'That's the lad!' said Tim, with a flash of his blue eyes. 'And here now! I've been keeping this half-crown for you. It should be more. I don't know where the money goes!'

'You gave Aunt Maureen a pound!' Shane told him. 'And I don't want the half-crown. You bought me this book when we were in Cork. That's enough!'

'And ye liked the book as much as ye thought ye would?' asked Tim, his face serious, though his eyes were still smiling.

The boy knelt up.

'I didn't know there were books like it. This must be the best book in the whole world!'

'I'm glad! I promised yer mother I'd look after ye. But I'm a scatter-brain! There, take the half-crown and don't read any more. I must sleep now for I've to be up before dawn.'

'I'll wake you!' promised Shane.

He could wake any hour he chose and, though a heavy mist had swept down from the mountains, Shane was awake and dressed before even his Aunt Maureen was about. He blew up the faint pink ash of the turf fire with the big clumsy bellows, piled on sods, and had the kettle boiling before she came out.

'Aren't you the good lad!' she whispered, so as not to wake the two smaller boys who were asleep on the settle bed. 'You even remembered the stirabout!'

Tim was still sleepy when he swallowed the last drop of his tea and stood up from the table.

''Tis the old mist!' he said, yawning. 'I'll be glad to feel the road under me feet!'

'Don't go mixing with the wild ones of Waterford!' his sister warned him. 'Good-bye now and don't stay away too long!'

'The moment the job's done I'll be on me way back!' declared Tim. 'Come on, Shane, if ye're coming!'

He strode along the muddy road, growing more awake and cheerful every moment. His legs were so long Shane had to run to keep up with him.

At the cross-roads a farmer was waiting with a herd of frisky bullocks.

'Ye're late, Tim Madden!' he shouted. 'The bastes is getting restless. I was afeard ye'd let me down!'

'Ye need never fear that, Mr Healy! I never let a man down yet and I never will!' declared Tim.

He slapped and whistled, pushed and coaxed, until the bullocks stood before him, orderly and obedient.

'No dog! No switch! Is it magic ye use on them?' asked the farmer. 'Ah, Tim Madden! 'Tis wasted on that mean bit of a starving farm y'are!'

'There's always the future!' cried Tim, with a broad grin. 'I'll bring the creatures along easy and steady. They'll be the pick of the Fair! I have half a dozen cows and a few sheep waiting on me at O'Connells and MacSharries, so I must be on me way!'

'Do yer best, Tim, and ye'll find I'm not a mean man!' the farmer assured him. 'Me brother will pay ye before ye leave the town.'

'Good-bye now, Mr Healy! I'll do me endeavours! No, Shane! Ye can't come a piece of the road with me. Maureen will be expecting ye back and ye wouldn't want to be late for the school. Safe home now! I'll be back tomorrow, or the next day by the evening bus. Watch out for me!'

'I'll be here!' promised Shane.

He climbed the wall to see the last of his uncle, strolling comfortably behind the trotting bullocks. When they disappeared into the mist beyond a clump of birch trees he dropped to the ground.

Mr Healy, who stood on the bank, winked at the boy.

'I'm afeard ye'll watch many a night for that laddo!' he chuckled.

Shane stared, only slowly understanding.

'Uncle Tim said he'd be back by the evening bus tomorrow or the day after. You heard him!'

'Not being deaf, I heard him. Oh, I heard! Me bastes are safe with Tim Madden. I know that! But he was born with a hole in his pocket. He'll be neighbourly with every stranger he meets and he'll buy presents for the family. When the money's finished, he'll be back, not before! And while he's in Waterford, he may find a job that will take him to Dublin.

One time he did that and twas three months or more before he turned up. Ye wouldn't remember! Ye were only a little chap. It wasn't long after ye both came to live with Joseph Keating. God help ye!'

'I do remember!' muttered Shane. 'I thought he'd never come back. I was frightened I'd never see him again.'

The farmer, looking at the boy's downcast face, was sorry.

'Don't mind the old chat I've been giving out!' he said. 'Tim mayn't be back tomorrow. He'll hardly do that even if he wants to. But he'll not stay away this time, not if he can help it. Only don't expect him too soon!'

'All the same, I'll be down to meet the evening bus to-morrow!' declared the boy. 'I promised!'

His shoulders hunched, he trudged back to the Keating farm.

4. The Drover who Didn't Come Back

The next night Shane was down at the cross-roads waiting for the bus. He was there long before it could be expected and he had slipped so quietly from the kitchen that only Maureen noticed his going. She smiled and shook her head. Tim wouldn't be back yet. But Shane was obstinate. He had said he would meet the bus every evening and he would.

It was better than staying in the farmhouse listening to Uncle Joseph finding fault.

Shane perched on the stone wall where he would see the bus coming round by Cloony's Wood.

'I won't look till I hear it!' he decided. 'But I won't let on before Uncle Tim gives a shout. He must be on it! He must!'

Shane tried not to be excited but, when the bus topped the rise, there he was down on the road, biting his lip, fists clenched, eyes watchful.

The bus slowed but did not stop.

Shane ran after it.

'Isn't Tim Madden with you?' he called.

The conductor, who knew all about Tim and Shane, swung out on the step.

'I heard he was in Waterford!' he shouted back. 'But I never set eyes on him!'

Shane leaned again the wall, shaken with disappointment.

He quickly recovered.

'I'd no right to expect him. Tonight or tomorrow, he said. He'll be here tomorrow and so will I. I couldn't bear to have Uncle Tim come and me not be here to meet him.'

Tomorrow went by, the next day, and the next. But no Uncle Tim!

Every evening Shane was at the cross-roads and every evening the bus went by without stopping.

'Don't fret yourself,' Aunt Maureen told him kindly. 'Tim always meant well but he never did know one day from another. Let him get with a crowd of lads, even if he'd never set eyes on them before, and night or day would be all the same to him. Terrible sociable is our Tim!'

'I'll try once more,' said Shane. 'Then he can come when he likes. I'll not be there!'

He dragged his feet along the boreen. Uncle Tim might have written, if only a postcard, that would show he remembered!

He didn't climb the wall. He had listened and watched so often he could tell the sound when it was no louder than the drone of a bee and see by the darkening of a distant tree when the bus was coming to the river.

There it was! The driver didn't slacken speed. He was sorry for Shane but he thought it foolish to encourage the boy. The conductor leaned out.

'No luck, lad!' he called. 'Best give him up!'

Shane forced a smile and waved his hand.

'How can I give him up?' he asked himself. 'Yet if Uncle Tim doesn't keep his word, what can I do?'

He despised the tears which came into his eyes.

'Crying! And me going on fourteen! I should be ashamed!'

Hands deep in his pockets, Shane turned back. As he drew near the back of the farmhouse he heard shouts and saw the children dancing round a bonfire.

'That's my bonfire!' he cried indignantly. 'I built it and I'm the one should light it!'

Tim had taught the boy to burn all the rubbish that couldn't be dug into the ground. He gathered twigs and leaves, cabbage stumps, old papers, rags, all the litter of the house and, as darkness fell, set fire to the heap. The ashes he dug into the garden and Aunt Maureen boasted that Tim's bonfires had made her onions the best for miles around.

At first Joseph was scornful. Lately he had changed and had used the ash for his gooseberry and blackcurrant bushes. But he declared it was to prevent the wind blowing the stuff into his eyes.

Shane started running, then stopped. Why shouldn't the young ones have the fun of lighting the fire? They helped him gather dry sticks and weeds, so hadn't they a right to start the bonfire?

He came slowly towards them. The boys were quarrelling. Suddenly he heard Maggie's shrill voice above theirs.

'Wait till Shane sees what you have done to his book, Des Keating! He'll have your life!'

Shane halted, then sprang forward, coming in a rush upon the startled group about the bonfire.

Des and Jer were struggling. Des held up a tattered book. Jer, on tiptoe, grabbing in one hand a few torn pages, tried to loosen his brother's grip. The bigger boy had the advantage. With a sudden thrust he pushed Jer away and rushed to the other side of the bonfire.

He hadn't noticed Shane's approach and bumped into his cousin.

'I never meant! I didn't go for to! Oh, Shane, I'm desprit sorry! We never wished to harm the book!'

Gazing at the other boy in dismay, he dropped the tattered red-and-gold cover. The cloth was torn, the cardboard stuck out. On the ground a black-and-white picture turned and twisted in the hot air from the blazing rubbish as if it were alive.

The two little girls drew near. Babs's face was streaked with tears. Maggie caught Shane's hand.

'We'll save all our money!' she declared. 'We'll buy you a better book, the best book in Cork. I told Des not to bring it out. He wanted to look at the pictures but he and Jer started fighting over it!'

'This was the best book in Cork!' muttered Shane. ' Twas Uncle Tim bought it for me – the last time we were there together.'

He knelt beside the fire and gently gathered up the crumpled pages. The thick black print stared up at him – *The Amazing Adventures Of Lemuel Gulliver*. There were the dwarfs of Lilliput, the giants of Brobdingnag, the noble horses. He remembered that day in Cork when Uncle Tim was buying presents for them all.

'And what can I give me bold comrade?' he asked, smiling around him at crowded Patrick Street and then down at Shane.

They stood outside a bookshop. The window was piled with old books in massive bindings. The doorway was narrowed by them. Uncle Tim was puzzled. Books! Books! Books! Sure you left them with all your other troubles behind you when you came out of the schoolhouse for the last time. Lessons! Scoldings! Slappings! God help the poor little divils who still have to go through it all! Yet here was young Shane, his eyes popping from his head and all because of a book in the dreariest shop in Cork!

Uncle Tim was kind and Shane was more like a brother than a nephew. He looked at the book again.

Amazing Adventures! Might be a story book! Nothing wrong with a good story told beside the fire of a winter night when a man was tired from a hard day at the Fair or on the land. Reading was different! Yet if the lad wanted it!

'Why not choose a new book?' he asked. 'Look! Over yonder! So new, they're sticky with the paint that's on them! You can see the colours from here!'

Shane looked.

'They're not books!' he cried. 'Not real books! There's nothing to read in them!'

Tim Madden pushed the boy into the shop before him.

'Hello, there!' he cried. 'Here's a lad wants a book, an old book that's stuck in the window!'

A tall old man stood up from behind the counter. He wore thick, heavy glasses low down on his nose and he looked at the young man and the boy over them.

'There are many books in the window!' he said.

'The one with the pictures!' hinted Shane.

The old man smiled at him.

'*Gulliver's Travels!*' he said. 'I envy you to be reading it for the first time. And you, young man!'

'I'm no reader!' Uncle Tim told him. 'But I can listen to a good story and Shane's the one who can tell a story. Just like the grandfather before him. I'm buying all the young ones presents and if Shane wants a book he shall have it!'

The old man brought the book out from the window. He wrapped it carefully and handed it over the counter.

'Good reading all the days of your life!' he said to Shane.

'And the price?' asked Uncle Tim, quite gently.

He had been spending gaily. Now he feared he would not have all the money the old bookseller was sure to want for his treasure.

'Oh, the price!' murmured the old man. 'The price!'

Tim laughed and his laughter filled the shop.

Suddenly the three of them were laughing as if they had heard the funniest story of their lives.

''Pon me word!' cried Uncle Tim. 'Isn't it very queer for a bookseller to forget asking the price for his book? You'd not do that if you dealt in cattle!'

He pulled out a ten-shilling note and laid it on the counter.

'Is that a fair price for Amazing Adventures?' he asked.

'It is indeed! It's more than enough! I'll find some change!'

The old bookseller pulled open a drawer.

'You will not!' said Uncle Tim. 'Good-bye now, and may we meet again! Out with ye, lad!'

And now the book Uncle Tim had bought him was torn and destroyed. Shane thought of that wonderful day in Cork. All that was left of it lay at his feet.

'Please don't be angry!' pleaded Des. 'I never thought. It's not hurt much. There's only a few pages burnt!'

Shane sprang up. He couldn't bear to see the torn cover and half-burned pages. Before Maggie could stop him, he flung the desolate little heap into the flames.

5. The Bonfire

As *Gulliver's Travels* flared up in crimson and gold flames Uncle Joseph came trotting up from the fields, carrying a hay fork across his shoulder. He saw the girls crying and Des trying to save the book from the flames. He changed his trot to a rush.

He pulled Des back from the bonfire, thrust in the fork, and raked out the unburnt scraps of the cover.

'Ye bold rascal!' he exclaimed. 'How dare ye destroy a perfectly good book!'

He shook Des so that the boy's head jerked backwards and forwards, and his hair fell over his eyes.

'I – I – d-didn't!' gasped Des. 'I didn't!'

'Twas me started it!' confessed Jer. 'Just for a bit of sport I took Shane's story-book. Des tried to snatch it from me and it got a wheeshy tear. Then Shane came up and he was real mad. Twas him threw it into the fire!'

Joseph Keating leaned on his fork.

'Is this true?' he asked Shane in amazement.

'It is!' answered Shane.

'Ye threw yer own book on the fire?'

'I did!'

'A perfectly good book and ye destroyed it?'

'It was torn and dirtied! I couldn't bear to look at it!' cried Shane, his voice breaking.

Jer and Des looked at one another sorrowfully.

'I wish I'd never touched the dirty old book!' spluttered Jer, and he wailed so loudly, Maureen came running out.

'Me poor child!' she cried. 'What ails ye?'

He tried to tell her, so did Des, so did Maggie. Joseph shouted at the top of his voice and Babs wept into her pinafore. Only Shane was silent.

'Shane threw his own book into the fire!' Aunt Maureen exclaimed at last. 'The one poor Tim bought him in Cork?'

She stared at the boy, her brown eyes shocked and amazed.

'Oh, Shane!' she said at last. 'How could you?'

'It was all spoiled!' he muttered. 'It wasn't like the book Uncle Tim bought me!'

How could he explain? Uncle Joseph raked the fire together while the others straggled into the house.

'Poor boy!' said Maureen to her husband. 'He's upset about not hearing from Tim. Don't scold him!'

'Scold him! Scold him!' exclaimed Joseph. 'I'd like to let

him feel the handle of this fork across his back! Tantrums at his age! I never heard the like!'

Shane filled a creel with turf and built up the fire. When the kettle was boiling, Maureen made the tea and called Joseph in, for he had gone back to the bonfire. He came slowly, shaking his head.

'I never did hold with books! But to go and destroy one, that's shocking!' he said, scowling at Shane.

'Sit down to the table all of you! And Joseph, leave the boy be!' ordered Maureen. 'He did a foolish thing and he's the one who'll suffer!'

The bacon was cold and fat but there wasn't anyone could make lighter soda bread than Aunt Maureen. The butter was rich and salty. Only Shane had no appetite.

'Here's a gorgeous crust!' whispered Jer, his eyes pleading and anxious. 'You have it!'

Shane pushed it away. He couldn't forgive Jer yet. He felt too miserable. He was glad when Joseph began to complain about the Kennedy's goats which were for ever trespassing on his land.

'A decent farmer doesn't keep goats!' he said indignantly. 'They're only fit for black heathens! I'll have the law on Charlie Kennedy before he's much older.'

'I wouldn't mind having a goat!' murmured Aunt Maureen. 'There'd be the milk!'

'I'd love a goat, so I would!' declared Des.

'Me too!' added Jer.

Maggie leaned back and looked from one face to the other. Nothing had been right since Uncle Tim went away! Why hadn't he come back? How could he leave poor Shane behind without a word? She looked at her cousin with sympathy but his head drooped and his mouth was pressed into a straight line.

Babs, sucking her thumb, leaned against her sister. Joseph Keating was still complaining about the goats.

'Mr Kennedy promised Tim he'd fix the hedge,' his wife told him. 'He'll surely do it!'

'I'll put the goats back where they belong!' declared Shane.

He marched out of the kitchen.

'I'll help, Shane! I'll help!' shouted Des, running after him.

The others followed, all anxious to console Shane. Uncle Joseph grinned, pulled his chair in to the table, and settled his elbows on it.

'Now I can have me tea in peace! Them young ones need managing. Shane may turn out quite useful, now he hasn't Tim to cock him up!'

'Shane's a good, hard-working boy, but how we'll manage without Tim's help I'm sure I don't know,' sighed Maureen, her face sad. 'Mind now, go easy with Shane! We don't want him going off on us! And he's a good, kind boy. Remember that!'

Uncle Joseph sniffed.

'That lad would never go off! Put Shane out the front door and he'd creep in at the back! I'll not deny he's a good worker. So was Tim for the matter of that. But he was discontented and always making the young ones long for things they couldn't have!'

Out in the field beyond the smouldering bonfire, Shane drove the Kennedys' goats towards the gap they had made in the hedge.

The old grey billy-goat, leader of the herd, tossed his head and, suddenly rearing up on his hind legs, danced towards the boy, horns curved, eyes glinting sideways, while the four other goats watched with mild interest.

He and Shane were old friends and loved a wrestle. But now the boy was serious.

'Get along with you!' he cried. 'Haven't I enough trouble without you starting your antics!'

The goat pranced. Des flung a clod of earth which fell short. Jer picked up a stone.

'Drop that!' shouted Shane. 'No need to be spiteful! The poor thing only wants a bit of fun!'

'Look at the horns on him!' protested Jer. 'I'm feard of me life of that one!'

Maggie ran behind the goat and caught his horns.

'Come along, old fella!' she said coaxingly. 'You must go home. Be a good boy!'

The goat was puzzled. He tried to shake her off, but she held firm, and slowly, step by step, the billy-goat allowed himself to be urged through the gap, his family following.

Only a small kid, not a month old, lagged behind, bleating timidly.

'Wish we could keep this one,' said Maggie. 'Why does dadda hate goats? I like them!'

'Best let it go with the others,' said Shane gently.

She let it go and it scampered gaily into its proper field.

Then Shane built up the gap with withered thornbushes, sods, and rocks. He stamped and pushed, the younger children helping. Babs brought stones and handfuls of grass. At last he was satisfied.

'Even old Billy won't be able to manage that!' he declared, gazing proudly at his work.

'He'll jump it!' warned Des. 'You couldn't raise a wall that would keep that one out!'

'Shane!' said Maggie earnestly. 'When you leave school, will you be a drover like Uncle Tim?'

Shane wrinkled his nose. He was thinking hard.

'If you're a drover, you should have a dog. Uncle Tim wanted one, but dadda doesn't like dogs, or cats either. Maybe he'd let you have one. I wish he would!'

The boys were rolling in the hay scattered around the stack. Shane stood kicking the turf, his hands in his pockets.

'I know what I must do when I leave school,' he said. 'I must go after Uncle Tim!'

'How will you find him?' asked Maggie. 'He's far away, most likely in Dublin.'

'All the more reason why I should seek him!' declared the boy. 'And why should I wait another three months? I'll go this very night!'

Maggie clasped her hands under her chin. Her brown pigtails stuck out on each side of her round, serious face.

'Oh, Shane! You daren't! What will dadda say?'

'He won't know till I'm gone! Promise you won't say a word!'

'I promise!'

'When will you go?' she asked in a thrilling whisper.

'When everyone's in bed and sound asleep. Mind now and don't let on!'

He smiled at her, gave a little nod, and walked into the house. Maggie stared after him.

Wasn't he the brave one! And he trusted her – not Des, or Jer but her – Maggie! Wouldn't it be grand when he and Uncle Tim came home together! She'd watch out, even if they didn't come for years and years. She'd watch the way Shane did!

6. Cross-roads and
Signposts

Shane had told himself to wake at twelve o'clock. But it was scarcely eleven when he was sitting up in bed.

What had roused him? What was that perched at the end of Uncle Tim's bed? Something white and glimmering, with big, staring eyes.

'Who are you?' whispered Shane, a shiver running from his head to his toes.

'It's me, Jer!' came the whispered answer.

'Go away! What do you want?'

'Dadda said I was to have Uncle Tim's bed. I waited till I thought you would be asleep. Mammy said you'd be lonesome.'

'And if I was lonesome for Uncle Tim, do you think you'd make up for him?' asked Shane fiercely, though still speaking in a whisper.

Jer shook his head.

'Then go out! Hear me? Go out!'

Jer didn't move.

'It's awful crowded for Des and me in the settle bed,' he ventured. 'And Uncle Tim wouldn't mind.'

Shane thought quickly. Maggie could keep a secret. Jer had to tell everything. No need to have him blamed for what he couldn't help.

'You can't come tonight,' he said. 'Tomorrow, maybe.'

'And you won't be mad to have me here instead of Uncle Tim?'

Shane rolled to the other side of the bed and pulled the blanket over his head. Jer crept out noiselessly, not making a sound even when he stubbed his toe.

Shane heard the kitchen door shut, then slipped from the bed and pulled on his clothes.

To his own surprise he was frightened. For the first time the darkness was terrifying. Yet he had come back from Cork in a thick mist. Even when he bumped into a cow and heard its protesting moo, he had only laughed. That time he fell in the river, and the other time when he had climbed the high elm to rescue Babs's balloon and the branch had crashed with him clinging to it, he hadn't felt a tremor. But Uncle Tim had been there, ready to push away the cow, to pull him from the river, to rub his bruised limbs. Even Uncle Joseph had praised him.

'The lad has spunk!' he said.

Shane thought how kind Aunt Maureen always was. If he waited, Uncle Tim would come back – one day!

He buttoned his coat, stuffed his muffler in his pocket, rolled his pyjamas, with his comb and tooth-brush inside them, in a crumpled sheet of brown paper. Then he emptied his money-box. Since he broke it open during the holidays he hadn't been able to save much. It was so easy to push up the lid. Still he had twelve pennies, two threepenny bits, one sixpence, and the half-crown Uncle Tim had given him. In the dim light he counted it quickly – four shillings and sixpence.

'Wish it was five shillings!' thought Shane.

To avoid going through the kitchen, where the boys slept, he climbed out of the window. Uncle Tim had made that window himself so that they could have plenty of fresh air. Uncle Joseph had jeered but Aunt Maureen was always wishing the rest of the windows were the same.

'A winda is to let in the daylight!' declared Uncle Joseph. 'If ye want fresh air, what's wrong wid opening the door?'

The east wind swept cold raindrops in the boy's face. They stung and freshened him. Gently he closed the window and stumbled down the boreen.

The gate opened easily. Uncle Tim had fixed it with new hinges just before he left. The smell of paint from the trellis Tim had made to train the pink roses, the sleepy clucking of hens from the new hen house, were all reminders of Tim Madden's energy.

'Wish he hadn't gone away!' said Shane to himself.

'No, I don't!' he added, feeling the easy steps of the stile. 'I'll show Uncle Tim I can manage alone.'

He tramped on, not bothering about ruts or puddles. He knew he wasn't managing alone. If he really wanted to do that, he would have stayed on at the farm and taken his uncle's place. Instead he was running after him, longing for his company and protection.

Reaching the second cross-roads, he found he was yawning and could hardly keep his eyes open.

Half asleep, he forced his tired legs through a tangle of briars and nettles to the shattered oak, which was quite hollow, though several limbs bore a thick crop of leaves and acorns. Inside it was warm and dry, the ground soft and powdery. Shane curled up, his head resting in a curve of the trunk. He drew a deep breath and at once began to dream he was propped against Uncle Tim while the young man told him the way to Dublin.

'Am I the kind of chap would stay in Waterford when the road to Dublin lies open before me? The road, a herd of the best bullocks from the Golden Vale, and a couple of lads who can sing a song, or tell a story with the best shanachie from West Cork!'

'Ah!' grieved Shane, smiling and stretching so that his feet struck against the smooth inside of the tree.

He did not wake but turned over and dreamed himself into a tangle of cross-roads and signposts to all the places he had ever seen or heard of. The sun rising over the Comeragh mountains woke him. An arrow of gold striking into the hollow of the tree filled it with light.

'Why wouldn't I make for Dublin if I don't come up with Uncle Tim in Waterford. Yet if he isn't in Waterford, I'd only be wasting me time going there and I might miss him altogether!'

Arguing with himself, he wriggled out of the tree and looked up at the signpost.

15 miles to Cork. 50 miles to Killarney. 20 miles to Waterford. 140 miles to Dublin.

He frowned, trying to decide which way he should go.

'A hundred and forty miles! That's a terrible long way! Every place is so far. I'd love to see Dublin! I'd be years getting there, unless someone gave me a lift!'

Uncle Tim was a great one for getting lifts. But he was a drover. He had a right!

'They'd ask me questions!' thought the boy.

Uncle Tim had promised that when they went to Dublin they would go by train. He had been so sure he would come back. What could have happened him?

The sun drew mist from the wet grass. Shane was hungry. He thought of the hot stirabout and the steaming tea they'd be having at the farm. There might be dripping toast for breakfast. If he did go back Aunt Maureen wouldn't be too hard on him for going out in the night. She'd understand.

Only Maggie would never again think him brave!

'All the same,' grumbled Shane. 'Why should I be brave? If Maggie thinks it all that easy, let her go and be brave herself!'

He turned his back on the signpost. The wind scattered showers of raindrops from the trees. He shivered and stopped again.

'It's a terrible rough road – all stones and mud! I should have followed Uncle Tim. He'd no right to go without me, not after all he said!'

He stood enjoying the warmth of the sun, sheltering from the wind and trying to make up his mind. Suddenly a roar like that of an angry bull startled him.

'There must be a drover on the road!' he thought, listening eagerly. 'Maybe he'd let me drive the beast. He might know Uncle Tim!'

Shane climbed the bank to see along the winding road.

A tall, thin old man, with long hair and a white beard which tossed like a flag, came striding along, striking the stones with a very knobby blackthorn.

'Where's the bull?' shouted Shane.

The old man came steadily towards him but did not answer.

Shane had not noticed before how the road twisted. Sometimes the old man appeared quite close. Then he moved away.

'That's why they call it the Corkscrew!' decided the boy.

When the old man came near again Shane called to him.

'Did you pass the bull and the drover or was it a runaway one?'

'Young eejit!' said the old man, without looking at him. 'Wait till I get round to ye!'

As he passed out of sight that terrible roar sounded so close Shane nearly fell from the bank.

'Run!' he shouted. 'Run! Don't let the bull come near you!'

The next time the old man came in sight he was chuckling.

'Such an eejit!' he said. 'I never met a worse!'

Shane's face became so red, he was thankful the old man's back was towards him, especially when a louder roar than before sounded from the road.

'Letting on to be a bull!' he muttered indignantly. 'Serve him right if a bull did come after him. I'll go on! If I go back I'd meet him!'

He went slowly on.

'I could have started after breakfast!' he was thinking, when a terrible roar close beside him sent Shane jumping.

'That gave ye a shock!' chuckled a wheezy voice, and there stood the old man.

Shane was so indignant he couldn't speak. He glared and the joker chuckled.

'No harm done!' he said. 'I always did like a bit of sport and I don't have as much fun as I used to. Have an apple to make up. Ye'll never put yer teeth into a juicier apple. Off the tree me own father planted the day I was born. Ripe and sweet, like me!'

Delighted with himself, he pulled from his pocket a big, red apple.

'There, lad!' he said, holding it out. 'No hard feelings! The best of friends, eh? Don't be cranky now!'

Shane was so angry he knocked the apple from the old man's hand and rushed away.

'Come back! Come back!' he heard. 'I meant no harm! I didn't mean to fright ye. Come back, ye bad-tempered young omadhaun! Don't be cranky!'

'Cranky!' thought Shane. 'Me cranky! I wouldn't take his apple if I was starving! And I'm not bad-tempered!'

7. Travelling People

Shane stopped at last. He had left the road and the rough track he followed crossed a boggy stretch between the mountains.

'I don't know these parts!' said the boy, looking back in bewilderment. 'I must have come miles and miles. Maybe Waterford is beyond the mountains. I wonder should I make for it!'

Heavy clouds hung on the horizon, though where he stood a shaft of sunlight turned the brown of the turf to gold. Pools bordered by forget-me-not and grey rocks glittered as if made of silver.

The gurgle of unseen streams, the scuffles and scurryings of hidden life, prevented him from feeling alone.

The last tattered scraps of mist were fluttering away. His eyes followed them.

'I'll get to the other side of the mountains!' he decided. 'Waterford must be somewhere over there.'

He tried to walk the way Uncle Tim had taught him, not running, not walking, but striking the ground with the ball of each foot, so that he was urged forward. His shadow ran before him. The sun was swiftly climbing overhead and the breeze had dropped. He looked about him for a spring.

'Never drink from a pool!' Uncle Tim had warned him. 'Never touch still water. Wait for the leaping spring!'

He waited until his mouth was dry and his head aching.

'I must have a drink!' he muttered, and kneeling down, was about to plunge his head in a clear brown pool which looked like freshly made tea.

A hand gripped him by the collar, and in the mirror of the water he saw three people – a man, a woman, and a little girl.

'Let go!' he spluttered, swinging round, wrenching himself free, and jumping to his feet.

Three friendly faces stared at him in amazement.

'Sure I meant no harm!' said the man. 'Only how could a young ignorant lad like ye know the danger there could be in a pool of bog water – sickness and cramps and fevers!'

'Mebbe he was thirsty!' put in the little girl.

'What's wrong wid a mug of freshly made tea?' asked the young woman, smiling. 'We're resting over yonder and ye're very welcome to share the bit we have. Come along, Danny and Mon.'

She began walking across the bog to where a thin ribbon of blue smoke rose from behind a group of rocks covered with brambles. The child caught Shane by the coat and tugged him along. The man followed, whistling contentedly.

'Pity we didn't save a few herrings from the basketful we were given yesterday,' he said, as they came round by the rocks to the fire. 'Sure there's nothing so tasty as herring!'

The young woman laughed and lifted a tin plate covering

a big frying pan perched on two bricks beside the fire. Four fish, brown and crisp, were frizzling there and the savoury smell made Shane conscious of his great hunger.

'Aren't ye the girl, Barb!' cried the young man.

'And there's one for the strange boy!' said the little girl, as proudly as if she had done the catching and the cooking.

'We had more than we wanted,' explained Barb. 'So I saved these.'

She pulled Shane down beside her and unwrapped a big pan loaf, already cut. She put each fish on a slice of bread and handed them round. There were three enamel mugs and one tin one. Barb used the tin one herself.

'She's like Aunt Maureen,' thought Shane. 'Kind and friendly.'

The herrings had small cuts on each side where pepper and salt had been rubbed in. At the farm they never had fresh fish, only kippers or dried cod when a fish peddler on a bicycle came that way.

'Have ye been on the road long?' asked Barb.

Shane frowned as he looked at her. The frown vanished before the eager interest in her eyes. But he did not answer.

'It makes no matter,' she said. 'I can see ye're new to this way of life. Ye don't want to talk to strangers. I do! I get tired of not talking. We've been on the road all our lives but Mon here wants to go to the school. We stayed up by Ballinasloe for over a month and she went to the school there. She cried when we came away, didn't ye, Mon?'

Mon's mouth was full, but she nodded.

'She had a lovely teacher, only a young girl. They kept a shop and everyone took turns at being shopkeeper. Everything had to be written in a book in Irish and English and the best boy or girl for the day had all that was left in the shop, sweets and biscuits and apples. Wasn't that a grand way to be learning?' demanded Barb, wiping the pan clean with a slice of bread and breaking the slice fairly in four.

'That's not learning, that's playing!' declared Shane scornfully.

'What harm, if she gets the bit of schooling!' said Danny. 'Now yerself, I make no doubt, has all the learning in the world!'

'I haven't any at all!' declared Shane crossly.

'I do love reading a story-book or a song-sheet,' confessed Barb.

'I had a wonderful book!' Shane told them. 'It's burnt now!'

'That's a shocking great pity!' exclaimed Danny. 'Was it an enemy or an accident?'

Shane glanced at their sympathetic faces.

'I'll tell you!' he said.

They settled themselves more comfortably around the big fire. Danny sprawled full length, reminding the boy of Uncle Tim. Barb clasped her hands about her knees and propped her chin on them. Mon curled up against her mother.

Shane told them all he had read of *Gulliver's Travels*. They enjoyed the story of the Kingdom of the Dwarfs and Shane stopped frowning. He felt happier than he had been since Uncle Tim went away.

'I'd only started reading about the Talking Horses,' he said. 'I wish I knew how it ended.'

'Talking Horses!' repeated Danny. 'I've often understood what they were saying. But I'm very ignorant, God help me!'

'Isn't it a terrible pity, such a grand book to be destroyed!' sighed Barb. 'Let's hope ye'll come across it another time.'

'What name did ye say is on yer uncle?' asked Danny.

'Tim Madden!'

'And he's a drover?'

'He is!'

'A long thin chap wid a grand head of red hair, a brown face, and blue eyes!'

'You know him?' cried Shane. 'You've met him? Where is he?'

He sprang up, looking from Danny to Barb.

Danny shook his head, laughing.

'Aren't ye a one for rushing a chap! No! I haven't met yer Uncle Tim. I haven't seen him. But I've heard tell of him. Oh, bedad! I've heard of him!'

'Where?' demanded Shane. 'Where?'

'Where but in Clonmel! That's the last town we were in, and that's where we heard of the mad young drover be the name of Tim Madden!'

'Uncle Tim isn't mad!' cried Shane angrily.

'Sure he isn't!' agreed Danny. 'A bit wild, but ye know the way people do be talking!'

Shane looked at him sideways.

'How could you hear of him in Clonmel when it was to Waterford he was going with a herd of bullocks and some sheep and maybe a few cows?'

Danny nodded.

'That settles it! This wild young drover had come from Waterford. There he came up wid a farmer who had three prize cows and wouldn't have them sold anywhere but in Dublin. And why not? Doesn't everyone know that tis there the best prices are given? There's yer man, on the way to Dublin. I reckon he's there by now. He was taking them on a lorry.'

'He might be on his way back! Go home and wait for him!' urged Barb. 'It's grand to have a home to go to.'

Shane made up his mind.

'Uncle Tim always had a great wish for Dublin. He wouldn't turn back the moment he got there. He'd stay as long as he could. I'll follow him!'

'Tis a terrible long way to walk!' said Danny. 'Now, if ye had the money, the train would take ye in a gallop and the sooner ye reach Dublin the more chance ye have of finding yer uncle.'

'A young lad like yerself would only need a half-ticket,' added Barb. 'But where would a poor boy without a father have the price even of a half-ticket? Ye should try for a lift!'

Shane felt the money in his pocket. Uncle Joseph always declared wandering people were thieves and robbers. But the boy knew he could trust these.

'I have four and six!' he told them. 'Would that be enough?'

Danny scratched his head. Barb shrugged her shoulders.

'Dublin's a shocking long distance!' muttered Danny.

'I wouldn't know what price they'd charge for taking ye there.'

'All the same, four and six is a deal of money!' said Barb. 'It should be plenty!'

'Have ye e'er a notion whereabouts in Dublin this same Tim Madden would be making for?' asked Danny. 'Tis a desprit big city. There's miles and miles of streets there. Ye'd need to have an address!'

'Of course I have an address!' cried Shane. 'The Cattle Market! Uncle Tim said he'd have friends there and they'd help him to a job when we got to Dublin!'

Danny grinned with relief.

'That settles it!' he declared. 'All ye need now is a station and a train. Clonmel's the place. Ye might even get news of yer uncle there. Yonder's the track, along be the Mountain of the Fairy Women. As ye come round it, ye'll see Clonmel wid the station and the trains. I wouldn't be surprised if ye're in Dublin before the night's over!'

8. A Lift to Dublin

Shane said good-bye to the travelling people. Barb was sure that a boy with four and six in his pocket would have no trouble in reaching Dublin. Danny thought he might be able to get a lift, but even if he had to tramp there it wouldn't do him a morsel of harm.

Shane had never been so alone before. Always there had been Uncle Tim or Aunt Maureen, or even his cousins. Now as he climbed along the slope of the mountain, the silence frightened him.

He turned to go back to Barb and Danny and Mon. Yet when he looked after them they were so distant they seemed small and strange. They were packing, too, and, as he stood watching, they hoisted their bundles and went out of sight.

Only Mon looked back. She didn't wave and Shane knew she couldn't see him. He was hidden in the shadow of the mountain.

His boots made so much noise on the rocks, he tried to tread on patches of moss and the short, fine grass growing in crevices. He whistled but after a few bars he fell silent.

'Not even a bird!' he muttered. 'This is a lonely place!'

He hurried on and, suddenly, heard the piercing scream of a train. Before him, at the foot of the mountain, huddled a town. He could see the roofs and, at the far side, beyond a wide, sparkling river, a pillar of smoke.

'That's Clonmel, and there's the station! Maybe I will be in Dublin tonight!'

Now Shane ran, and he was a quick runner. He raced through the town and reached the station while porters were still lifting luggage from the van.

He had never bought a railway ticket before.

'I want a half-ticket to Dublin, please!' he said to the sharp face which looked out at him from the square hole.

'Second class – that will be ten and eightpence halfpenny, if ye're under fourteen. Ye look a size large for that!'

'I am under fourteen but I've only four and six!' protested the boy.

'Then go back home and tell yer da, or yer mammy, and let them give ye the rest of the money. But don't be blocking the way for decent people who can pay for their tickets!' growled the ticket man.

Shane could see the doors of the carriages opening and slamming a few yards away. He wondered if he could slip by the fat man in uniform who was clipping the tickets, dash across the platform, and leap into a carriage as the train moved off. But he did not stir and it rumbled slowly away out of sight.

A boy, little older than himself, kept step with Shane as he wandered out of the station.

'Did I hear ye say ye had four and six?' he asked.

Shane stared at him crossly.

'What business is it of yours?'

'If ye want to get to Dublin, I can put ye in the way of it – for four and six!'

'And what will I do there without a penny in me pocket?'

'Ye'll be no worse off than if ye went there by train.'

Shane stared at him in silence.

'Why do ye want to go to Dublin?' demanded the boy curiously. 'People there? Friends? Running away?'

'I'm looking for my uncle. He was going to take me to

Dublin with him when he came back from Waterford and he hasn't come back!'

'He went to Waterford, so ye've come to Clonmel to folly him to Dublin. Ye're a quare one! Look now! Give me a shilling for meself and sixpence for chips. I'll share with ye, and I'll get ye on a lorry that's making for the Dublin Cattle Market in half an hour. I'm sorry for ye and I don't mind doing a chap a good turn!'

Shane stared doubtfully at the boy's peering eyes.

'Where's the lorry?' he asked.

'Give me the money and I'll fix ye up! If ye can't trust me to the tune of a dirty old shilling, ye can walk to Dublin for all I care!'

Shane looked about him. The station was almost deserted but in a yard close by were two lorries, one empty, the other loaded with sheep whose protesting baa-aas came faintly on the wind.

'What's to stop me climbing up there?' he thought. 'I don't need help for that!'

The boy guessed what Shane was thinking.

'Ye wouldn't go for to cheat me?' he asked. ' Twouldn't do ye a ha'p'orth of good! I'm no stranger here. Everyone in Clonmel knows Jimsy Nolan. And d'ye think the old watch-dog will let ye set foot in the yard?'

He nodded towards the collie, which, fastened to the empty lorry, raised its head and sniffed suspiciously at every passer-by.

'If it was dark I'd take a chance!' Shane told himself. 'Why shouldn't I wait until night and try for a lorry then?'

But he was too impatient to wait. He was sure he would find Uncle Tim in Dublin and he longed to be on his way there.

'Here's a shilling!' he said, reluctantly holding it out.

Jimsy Nolan snatched it.

'Where's the sixpence for chips?' he asked. 'Ye'll need a bite!'

Shane had eaten chips in Cork. The memory made him hungry.

'I'll come with you!' he said.

'Ye'll do as I say or ye won't get near that lorry!' cried Jimsy Nolan indignantly. 'Is it a miser y'are? Aren't ye real mean to grudge a poor lad a few old coppers! I heard what ye were told at the station – ten and eightpence ha'penny for a ticket to Dublin. I'm saving ye a fortune and ye want to rob me of a mouthful of chips!'

'Oh, here you are!' exclaimed Shane.

Jimsy Nolan snatched the sixpence, darted across the main street, and vanished down a narrow alley beside the West Gate.

Shane propped himself against the wall, studied the quiet street, looked beyond to the mountains, and decided to go in search of his new acquaintance. As he crossed the road he looked back and saw two men striding towards the station.

'Wonder if they're lorry men!' considered Shane.

But they passed into the main street from where, long ago, his Aunt Maureen had told him, before the railway was built, the Bianconi long cars – the first stage coaches in Ireland – set out on their journeys.

Shane was wondering would he see Jimsy Nolan again when he heard a shout and there was the boy racing towards him.

'Ye'll have to hurry!' he panted as he reached Shane. 'The lorries is starting early. I'll go first and do ye let on to be chasing me. When there's no one looking, I'll give ye a leg-up and keep the dog quiet. Folly me close!'

He ran across the road and back again. Shane kept up with him easily, dodging the leisurely traffic and ignoring the angry voices of foot passengers who were forced to step out of their way.

Shane soon grew tired of saying 'Sorry, ma'am!' and 'Pardon, mister!' and stayed on the side of the road nearest the station.

The yard where the lorries stood was still deserted. The dog came to the length of his chain but allowed Jimsy to stroke him and didn't growl.

'I'd as well get up now!' suggested Shane.

'And be found!' cried the other. 'The driver will make sure all is safe before he starts – they always do! He wouldn't have to look far to find ye!'

'Where's the chips?' demanded Shane.

'I'll get them! I saw the chaps come along and ran to warn ye! I thought they'd be here by now. Where can they have gone?'

'I saw them too!' Shane told him. 'They went down along there.'

'Here they come!' whispered Jimsy. 'Let on we're having a bit of a scrap!'

He gave Shane a push. Shane pushed back, a little harder than he intended and sent Jimsy staggering so that he fell against the loaded lorry.

'Clear off!' shouted the older of the men. 'You lads are a pest! You'll never be happy till you're run over! Keep away from the lorries. I'm warning you!'

The boys retreated.

'Aren't you the eejit!' muttered Shane. 'I'd have done better by myself!'

Jimsy rubbed his nose.

'Let ye wait! I'll stand by ye. I'll see ye righted! I'll not stir from this place till ye're tucked away safely!'

They strolled a little way. Without looking, Shane knew that the driver was getting ready. Presently the older man, having made sure the sheep were safe, said farewell to his companion and went off.

'Now!' whispered Jimsy.

They went quietly into the yard. The driver was busy with his engine and, concealed by the body of the lorry, Shane seized a loop of rope and swung himself over the back.

The dog barked and rattled his chain.

'Quiet!' ordered the driver, without raising his head.

'Is there room?' asked Jimsy, speaking very softly.

'Heaps!' murmured Shane.

Indeed he was surprised at his luck. A wooden barrier kept a narrow space free of the sheep. A heap of clean sacks were folded there, making a rough bed where he could lie at full length or sit propped up as he pleased.

'As good as the train?' whispered Jimsy.

Shane nodded.

'Then give me another three bob!'

'Three bob!'

Shane formed the words with his lips but made no sound.

'Three bob!' repeated Jimsy.

'No!' said Shane, very distinctly.

'Then I'll tell the driver!'

Jimsy moved away but his eyes were fixed on the other boy's face.

'It's worth it!' he added.

'I can walk to Dublin!' thought Shane.

Yet he might reach the city after Uncle Tim had left it. He decided quickly, pulled out his three shillings, and dropped them into Jimsy's outstretched hand.

Jimsy dashed away as the driver stepped back, wiping his oily hands.

'Hi, you!' shouted the man. 'What divilment have you been up to?'

He walked slowly round, surveying his lorry. The dog growled.

'A grand watch-dog you are!' grumbled the man.

The collie wagged its tail. The sheep baa-ed.

'No harm done!' muttered the driver. 'And you can't keep lads away from lorries!'

He strolled to the front. A man came up from the back of the yard.

'All fixed?' he asked.

'All fixed!'

'I'll be seeing ye!'

'Ye will indeed! Tomorrow night!'

The motor throbbed. Shane knelt up cautiously and peered out.

'Duck down!' said a sharp voice. 'Here's the chips!'

A greasy bundle was thrust up at him. He grabbed it as an orange was flung after.

'Good luck!' he heard, through the clatter of the engine and the rattle of heavy wheels over cobbles.

9. Dublin Cattle Market

Shane nibbled the chips slowly. They were crisp and hot in their wrapping of paper. Jimsy had eaten only a few from the sixpennyworth and, though he had taken every bit of his money, Shane felt no anger towards him.

This was the journey he had dreamed of and, though he was alone, he was sure he would find his uncle at the end of it.

The orange was sweet and juicy. Shane clasped his hands about his knees and settled himself comfortably.

The lorry stopped twice but Shane's eyes were closed and he was dreaming. He didn't rouse until the bellowings, baa-ings, and moos of hundreds of beasts announced that he had arrived at the Dublin Cattle Market. It was scarcely dawn but powerful lights flooded the huge square inside the high railings.

Bewildered, between sleeping and waking, Shane lay blinking until the lorry lurched to a stop. He peeped over the side, watched his chance, and, grabbing his bundle, scrambled to the ground as the lorryman elbowed his way to the back.

The air throbbed with deep bellowings, plaintive baas, calm, indifferent mooings. Shane looked over a sea of animals surging through openings in walls and fencings.

Shane had never before seen so many animals together in one spot. The noise bewildered and excited him too. If he could find his uncle here it would be the most wonderful day of his life.

Following the crowd of boys, men, and dogs, he gazed eagerly at each drover, hoping to see Uncle Tim's red head and dancing blue eyes.

There were red heads and blue eyes in plenty but there wasn't a glimpse of his young uncle. When a good-natured looking drover halted beside him for a moment and wiped the dripping sweat from his face with the sleeve of his coat, the

boy ventured to ask: 'Do you know a drover by the name of Tim Madden?'

The man half-closed his eyes, scratched his chin, tossed up his switch and caught it again.

'I know a good score Tims and as many Maddens but ne'er a Tim Madden!' he answered at last.

The next one Shane asked advised him to go to a huge dealer who stood, check cap over one eye, in the centre of a sea of sheep, calling names, numbers, and prices steadily.

'I'd never get near him,' decided the boy. 'And he'd only run me if I did!'

Shane hadn't dreamed there were so many sheep and cattle in all Ireland. The sheep had great patches of red or blue on their wool. Some of the cattle were wild, shaggy creatures others so elegant they seemed like big toys. There were sheep with huge, curved horns and sheep with none at all.

Men lounged with cigarettes between their lips and switches under their arms. Others, coatless, filled pails from taps jutting out from the tops of upright pipes. He was pushed and thrust aside. Cows trying to force their way between groups of sheep bumped him gently. Bullocks, becoming restless, stood on their hind legs and butted one another. There were men on platforms shouting steadily, but the din was so great Shane couldn't understand a word.

'Uncle Tim could be here without us setting eyes on one another,' he thought.

The moment a drover, a dealer, or any man who looked the least friendly, stepped out of the crowd, Shane was beside him.

'Do you know a drover by the name of Tim Madden?' was his persistent question.

By midday, when the boy was seen approaching a fresh comer, the cry went up:

'Here's the lad seeking the lost drover!'

He was hungry again and tried to earn a meal by helping with the animals but no one wanted him. Too many boys were helping already.

'That Jimsy was a mean one to force every penny from me!' he thought resentfully. 'Wish I had some more chips!'

Using his hands as a cup, he drank water from a bucket left before a disdainful cow. He was so weary he longed to sit down. But there was scarcely standing room in the market and he was tired of being pushed and told to 'get along out of that!'

He hated leaving the one place where he had a chance of finding Uncle Tim or of meeting someone who knew him. Yet slowly he drew away from the noise and confusion until he found himself going down a winding street towards the river.

Now he saw drovers taking cattle away from the market. Big men, in loose tweed coats, stood on the steps of tall houses talking at the tops of their voices though there was little noise. One of the drovers, a muddy, tattered creature, was singing. Shane had heard his uncle sing that song many a time:

> '*Me father was a farmer*
> *Away beyond Ardloo.*
> *He wanted me, his only son,*
> *To be a farmer too.*
>
> *I had no wish for horses,*
> *For forks, or spades, or ploughs,*
> *I wanted for to see the world*
> *And not be milking cows.*
>
> *He sent me off to Kerry.*
> *I ran away to Cork.*
> *From there I went across the sea*
> *To the city of New York.*
>
> *But now I'm growing wiser*
> *And sadder too, ochone!*
> *I wish I had the heart and cash*
> *To cross the seas for home.*'

Shane ran after the man and the three bullocks he was driving.

'Hi, mister!' he said. 'Do you know Tim Madden?'

The drover was making so much noise Shane had to repeat his question three times.

At last the man turned his head, saw Shane, and winked.

'Well, lad! What is it? A penny because yer da's gone to England and yer mammy wants a sup of tay, or it's collecting ye are for a charity and no flags to show what an honest boy

y'are?' he chuckled. 'Ah, don't
be raging! I'm only joking!
Here's the penny and wel-
come!'

'I'm not asking for a penny!'
declared Shane proudly. 'I'm
asking do you know my Uncle
Tim. It's his song you're singing. Tim Madden, he is!'

The drover kept trotting
behind his bullocks and Shane
kept trotting with him.

'Is it know Tim Madden,
Tim Madden the drover from
Ballylicky! Is that what ye're
axing me?'

'It is!' replied Shane. 'You
know him?'

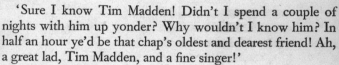

'Sure I know Tim Madden! Didn't I spend a couple of
nights with him up yonder? Why wouldn't I know him? In
half an hour ye'd be that chap's oldest and dearest friend! Ah,
a great lad, Tim Madden, and a fine singer!'

'Where is he?'

The drover frowned.

'How would I know where he is? I'm not his jailer!'

'When did you last see him? He's me uncle and I'm looking
for him. Do tell me!' pleaded Shane.

The man shut one eye.

'Would he be wanting ye to find him? that's the question.
Will I be doing the chap a good turn or a bad one if I put ye
on his trail? That's what I'm after axing!'

'Uncle Tim would want me to find him!' declared Shane.
'He always said we'd go away together when I'd finished with
school. I was waiting for him to come back from Waterford.
He didn't come, so I set off to look for him. I heard he'd come

to Dublin, so I came too. I thought he'd be at the Cattle Market, but he isn't there.'

By this time they had come to Blackhall Place, the bullocks were straying from one side of the road to the other, so that motor horns were warning them, and the tattered drover went so slowly Shane grew more and more impatient.

'Twas three days or more since I was wid Tim Madden!' said the man at last. 'We said good-bye on Eden Quay as the sun was rising over Dublin Bay and I have it in me mind he was making for the North Wall!'

'The North Wall!' cried Shane. 'Where's that? What would he be wanting there?'

'What does any chap want at the North Wall?' retorted the drover. 'Isn't that where the Liverpool boats come in!'

He nodded cheerfully, waved his switch, gathered his three bullocks together, and marched on, singing:

> *'I'm a Tipperary drover.*
> *I've tramped the country over,*
> *Through rain and fog*
> *O'er miles of bog,*
> *By mountain and by valley.*
>
> *An now me journey's ended,*
> *Be moon an stars befriended.*
> *Tonight I'll meet old friends galore.*
> *We'll drink each toast and then, one more,*
> *Down wid the Widda Nally.'*

Shane stood gazing after him, then followed down to the river. He saw a cart filled with little white turnips going along the quay. At every bump a few turnips were spilled out and Shane picked them up. When his pockets were filled, he sat on a step and began to eat. They were as sweet as apples and though he would have preferred them boiled with a piece of mutton and onions, his hunger was lessened.

He walked on past the Four Courts, stopping to admire the

great grey buildings and the mighty dome rising into the pale clear air. Men in queer white wigs and black untidy gowns strolled on the stone paths. Others in neat black hurried by them, carrying heavy volumes and looking very important.

When he saw women with boxes on wheels and men driving yokes up a side street he followed and so came to the vegetable market.

Other boys were earning money for lifting sacks of potatoes, holding horses, guarding motors, running messages.

Shane tried to find work too but it was no easier here than at the Cattle Market. He was a stranger and he was late. He picked up some soft bananas which had been thrown away, then toiled back to the Cattle Market.

The cows and sheep, the dealers and drovers were gone, the farmers had finished their buying and selling. The big, empty place, with its littered cattle pens, was being cleaned and the few men there were willing to listen to the boy's questions.

Some knew Tim Madden and thought they had seen him a few days ago but not one could tell where he had gone. Shane felt it was foolish to stay there, though each time he wandered away he was drawn back.

That night he found shelter under an empty crate in a deserted yard. A storm of wind and rain kept him awake and he was thankful when grey dawn came over the quiet city.

He began to think of going back to the farm.

'Aunt Maureen would be glad to see me again,' he thought.

But he dreaded Uncle Joseph's jeers as much as he disliked leaving this great city he had longed for all his life.

If only he had a friend or could find work. He dared not look forward to another night without food or shelter.

He went down to the river and leaned upon the wall, looking enviously at the swans and sea-gulls.

'They find plenty to eat!' he thought.

He could not keep still and walked on.

At a corner he saw a shop window crammed with books. Over the door he read in faded gold letters:

THE FOUR MASTERS' BOOKSHOP

He thought of the book Uncle Tim had bought him that happy day in Cork and went across.

Propped open in the window was a big book with black-and-white pictures.

'*Gulliver's Travels*,' he read, and went on reading.

10. The Four Masters' Bookshop

Shane sat up in bed, a strange bed. Beside him lay a boy with dark hair and eyebrows raised, so that even in sleep his face had a surprised look. One fist was clenched under his chin, the other flung above his head.

'Spose I'm lucky! Ought to be thankful!' thought Shane.

Slowly he remembered all that had happened since he stood looking in at the bookshop window.

He tried not to think of yesterday, only of what he must do today. He pulled on his clothes and went from the room. At the top of the stairs he stood and gazed down at two startled faces looking up at him.

'I forgot country boys always rise early,' said Mr O'Clery with a smile.

Mrs O'Clery beckoned.

'Come down and have a cup of tea!' she told the boy. 'Tuck into the soda bread! It's good, solid stuff! Mrs Flanagan makes it and she comes from West Limerick where they know good food. Use plenty of butter. It's farmer's butter with a real taste on it!'

Shane smiled gratefully at her. She wasn't a bit like his Aunt Maureen, who was always flustered and untidy in the mornings, but she had the same kind ways.

'Were you dreaming of your uncle?' she asked.

He nodded.

'Yes, ma'am!'

He no longer minded being questioned, not by these people.

'Thought I'd go up to the Cattle Market,' he mumbled. 'Might hear some news!'

He was hungry and there was a rich nutty flavour in the bread.

'If you don't find your uncle, come back!' Mr O'Clery told him. 'In any case, let us know!'

Two big cups of strong tea with plenty of creamy milk, as much white sugar as he liked from the big blue basin, three cuts of soda bread, a wash in cold water in the ramshackle bathroom beyond the kitchen, and Shane was eager to be out in the Dublin streets, continuing his search.

He helped the bookseller unbolt the door.

'You know your way?' asked Mrs O'Clery, half-doubtful.

'I was there yesterday and the day before!' came the answer, as Shane went out into the grey misty morning.

'I wonder where he slept that other night!' she murmured, staring after the boy, who lingered to look across at the towers of Christ Church rising out of the mist which lay thick on the river.

'I should have thanked them!' thought Shane. 'I wouldn't want another night under that crate! But what will I do now if there's no trace of Uncle Tim? Where can he have gone?'

He went along the quays. The pavement was wet, though the roofs and towers across the river were beginning to sparkle as the sun rose high.

The moment Shane left the bookshop behind he began to feel anxious. The pavement was crowded but he dared not try the roadway, for buses, motors, and cyclists took up every inch. He could not run. Hurrying was useless and by the time he reached Blackhall Place he was almost convinced that this delay would prevent him from finding Uncle Tim.

The road leading uphill to the Cattle Market seemed a leisurely friendly place after the confusion of the quays. As he came out on the North Circular Road, with its avenue of trees reaching one way to the Phoenix Park and the other way to a church soaring high above Dublin, Shane saw the Cattle Market stretching huge and empty.

At first he thought it was quite deserted. Then he heard the melancholy baa-ing of sheep and went forward to where a few flocks were being sold by a man standing up above the dealers and drovers grouped around.

Some of the sheep were grander than any Shane had seen before. Their fleeces were pure white and very short. They stood, listening proudly to the auctioneer.

'Fifteen guineas for one ram lamb!' muttered Shane. 'I don't believe it! But he's lovely! He's worth it all, every penny!'

He walked along the pens, admiring the occupants – white sheep, yellow sheep, lambs like beautiful toys, haughty and elegant rams with close-curled horns. Pure bred; of course they were! Each one deserved a prize!

In a pen by themselves were two dozen shaggy, long-legged, dirty sheep, who baa-ed incessantly. Shane felt more at home with these. Though when he greeted them and explained where he came from, they looked past him with their bleak, indifferent eyes.

A sheep-dog, idling because his master was idling, strolled over to the boy, rubbed against him, and licked his hand.

'Hallo, old chap! You're the kind of dog I'll have one day!' said Shane, stroking the smooth, narrow head and feeling pleasure in the dog's friendliness.

He followed when a drover, leaning over the rail of a pen, a switch twisting in his fingers, his tattered old cap at the back of his head, whistled to the dog.

'Well, lad!' said the drover. 'If ye're a friend of my friend

Patch, I'm pleased to make yer acquaintance! Up with the dad?'

'I'm looking for my uncle, Tim Madden!' said Shane.

The man laughed.

'I've heard about ye, lad! So ye're looking for poor Tim Madden?'

'You've seen him!' cried Shane. 'When? When did you see him? Where is he?'

The man pushed his cap back a little farther until it was a wonder it didn't fall off.

'I met him – once!' he said. 'A lively chap! A good drover, I reckon!'

'Where was it? Where is he now?'

'Last Wednesday week! He brought in a lorry-load of cows, fine beasts they were too. I gave him a hand though twasn't much help he needed. Great company, he was! I wouldn't mind meeting Tim Madden again, so I wouldn't!'

'Where is he now?' repeated Shane. 'I'm looking for him! I've come all the way from Ballylicky to find him!'

'How would I know that? There's some come here week after week and I never even know their names. Yer uncle's different. But I couldn't say where he is now!'

'Where did he go?' asked the boy, beginning to despair. 'Will he come back?'

'I couldn't rightly say. But this I do know! He went off with an eejit that was staying along there in Stoney Batter and let on he was lonesome. Lonesome – how are ye! If ye could find that chap, he might tell ye more!'

'You don't know the house?'

'Deed and I don't! I've told ye all I know. There's not many houses in Stoney Batter. It's down along there. Ye'll find the place easy and I hope ye find the man!'

'Hi! Shane Madden! Over here! Shane Madden!'

Shane swung round. He almost hoped to see his uncle's red head and laughing eyes. Almost as welcome were Patrick and Bridgie, who stood clinging to the railings of one of the pens. He ran over to them.

'Any luck?' asked Patrick.

'That drover saw Uncle Tim last Wednesday. He went off with a man who was staying in Stoney Batter. I'm going there now! I'll knock at every door till I get news of him!'

'You're to come home to dinner!' Bridgie told him. 'Isn't the dirty market clean today, now there's nobody here!'

'I'll find Uncle Tim first!' declared Shane.

'The dinner's ready!' Patrick told him. 'You can go after!'

Shane hesitated.

'Suppose I missed him because I put dinner first!' he said.

'It can't make all that difference!' objected the other boy. 'Me mother will be sorry if you don't come. We'll go the short cut down North King Street, and you can come back as soon as we've finished!'

Bridgie tugged Shane's hand.

'There's fried whiting and chips and carrots. It's a lovely dinner! Mrs Flanagan will be real vexed if we're not there when she takes it up and I won't go without you. I'll help you find your uncle after school. You knock one side of the street and I'll knock the other!'

'Better come!' advised Patrick.

Shane wanted to go on with his search yet he dreaded another disappointment.

'Mebbe it won't make a deal of difference!' he muttered.

Patrick started running to give the strange boy less time to change his mind. When they reached the bookshop, Shane, to his surprise, felt he was coming home. The bookseller's nod, Mrs O'Clery's welcoming smile, made him glad he wasn't knocking at closed doors and discovering he was too late.

Mrs Flanagan sat down at the table with them and looked with sympathy at Shane.

'Did ye hear tale or tidings of the uncle?' she asked.

Shane told all he had found out.

'Stoney Batter!' she cried. 'Is it Stoney Batter? And it a house where there were drovers! Then ye've no need to go hunting! Tis Mrs MacNally's boarding-house ye're wanting! The third on the left-hand side going up to the market. A clane, dacent-looking house it is, wid white lace curtains to every winda. Eat up now! If anyone can tell what's happened yer poor, misfortunate uncle tis Mrs MacNally! She's a widda like meself, God help her! Her husband was a drover, so she has a kindness for that class of chap. Ask her all ye want to know and she'll tell ye! Say ye're acquainted wid the Widda Flanagan and she'll see ye righted!'

'You're terrible good!' said Shane, feeling as if Uncle Tim was only round the corner. 'I don't know how to thank you!'

'No thanks required, me poor child!' she answered. 'I like a lad wid a bit of heart in him!'

This time Shane had a chair to himself. He felt so comforted about his uncle that he ate slowly and steadily, wondering when he would see him. The talking ceased. The only sound came from Mog, who miaowed crossly, demanding his dinner. At last Shane looked up, to discover the others had finished and were waiting for him. He became confused and could eat no more.

Bridgie was delighted.

'There, Mog!' she said. 'Shane was the only one who thought of you. You will have a feed!'

She and Patrick drank a cup of tea standing and ran off to school.

'They should have washed their hands when they came in!' exclaimed Mrs O'Clery. 'I forgot to tell them.'

'No need to worry about Patrick!' the widow assured her. 'He's for ever washing himself. But that young one hasn't learned yet what a tap is for.'

She gathered up the dishes and took them into the kitchen, followed by Mog. Shane stood up, eager to learn what had become of Uncle Tim, yet reluctant to leave this pleasant room.

'There's one thing I must ask,' said Mrs O'Clery. 'Did you come away without your aunt knowing?'

'I did!' answered Shane.

Mrs O'Clery shook her head reproachfully.

'That poor woman will be worried to death! First her brother goes off, then you. Isn't it a pity you didn't leave a note?'

'I never thought!' murmured Shane. 'I did tell Maggie. Only she promised she wouldn't let on. Maggie's one you could trust. Still, she's only a little girl, like Bridgie! She might tell!'

Mrs O'Clery laughed.

'If Bridgie promised not to tell, she just wouldn't, so if Maggie is like her, sit down at that table and write to your aunt! Here's paper and envelope. You can use my pen. Tell her where you are – the Four Masters' Bookshop, Ormond Quay, Dublin, that you're safe and she needn't worry.'

Shane sat looking down at the paper.

'Aren't you fond of her? Don't you mind her being worried?' Mrs O'Clery asked reproachfully.

The boy raised his eyes.

'It isn't that, ma'am! Only I've no right to be here! If you'd let me work, it would be different. I'll do anything – anything at all, and when I find my Uncle Tim, I'll be able to pay you back.'

Mrs O'Clery put her hand on his shoulder.

'You shall have work. We need you badly. Patrick is too young. You'll be a great help. Write your letter. Post it on the way to Stoney Batter. Then come back and start work.'

'You don't think I'll find me uncle, do you, ma'am?' asked Shane.

She looked at him thoughtfully.

'I don't think you'll find him today. But he can take care of himself. Go on with your own life and, when you do find him, have a welcome ready.'

Shane took up the pen. Mrs O'Clery went out to the shop. The Widow Flanagan came in from the kitchen and stood looking over his shoulder.

'There's the young scholar!' she cried in admiration. 'Ah, but ye're not the grand writer Patrick is! Put side by side wid him, ye wouldn't be bothered looking at the Book of Kells. Every letter a picture, especially the big fellas! That's Patrick! Is it to the auntie down in Ballylicky ye're writing?'

'It is!' replied Shane.

'Good lad! Good lad!' she told him.

'Mrs Flanagan! I'm going to work in the shop!'

'Now isn't that grand! Haven't I told them time and time again – ye need a shop boy! That's what I'm always after telling them. Though indeed, that wasn't in me mind at our first meeting. Wasn't I the eejit? Heaven help me!'

'Mrs Flanagan!' Shane spoke softly and his face turned very red. 'Mrs Flanagan! I'm going to work in the shop but I haven't a stamp to put on me Aunt Maureen's letter. Would you lend me the price of it? I'll pay you back as soon as I can.'

'Would I lend ye the price of a stamp to put on yer auntie's letter! That I would wid a heart and a half, only there's no need. Over yonder on the desk is a box of odd stamps and we just help ourselves. But ye'll need a few coins to rattle in yer pocket!' she went on with a laugh. 'Here's a shilling to go on wid and before ye're much older I'll have them fix ye a proper wage. They'd never think of it. God help them! They've read so many books they're fair moidered! If twasn't for me, every book in the shop would be lifted from under their noses and they'd never know! Are ye off to Stoney Batter?'

'I am, and thank you very much for your kindness!'

'Ye're very welcome,' she told him. 'I'll lave ye now to finish the writing.'

Shane was sticking a stamp on the letter as he went into the shop. He was so excited he blundered against a loaded table and knocked a pile of books to the floor.

Stooping to pick them up, he saw Mrs O'Clery sitting near the quay window, a book propped open before her. She read and knitted steadily at the same time, smiling as she considered the printed words. The boy stood, watching and wondering. She had his aunt's kindness but she seemed quite unaware of her surroundings.

Already Shane liked her. He wished she knew Aunt Maureen and he wished his busy, overworked aunt had the chance to sit and read, to look out upon the rushing world as calmly as Mrs O'Clery. He longed to tell the bookseller's wife about his aunt. But not now.

At the other side of the shop Mr O'Clery was perched on top of a step-ladder, a heavy book with small print and yellowed pages on his knees. He was frowning as he read.

Two men were looking at the books on the shelves. Shane hesitated. Should he ask them what they wanted? They seemed at home, so he left them and went out of the shop.

The quays were quiet. Only the mewing of sea-gulls and the hooting from a barge on the river disturbed the air.

'I'm going to work in the Four Masters' Bookshop!' the boy told himself. 'Won't Aunt Maureen be proud when she reads me letter! What will Uncle Joseph say? I wish Uncle Tim could know I'm going to work in the Four Masters' Bookshop!'

11. MacNally's of Stoney Batter

Shane went gaily along Arran Quay and up through Smithfield until he came to Stoney Batter. This was the road St Patrick had taken on his way from the North when he crossed the river by the Ford of the Hurdles.

Shane thought of that other boy, poor, lonely, a runaway slave. There were no houses then, only a ford across the river and clumps of nut bushes scattered about. Yet he, too, found friends.

The houses had high steps up to the doors. Shane remembered – the third on the left-hand side, the one with a printed card in the window – MRS MACNALLY'S BOARDING HOUSE.

There it was! He went up to the door and was about to knock when it opened and a woman, so broad she filled the doorway, stood looking at him. Her face was round and red. She wore a black dress and a white apron as large as a sheet. She clutched a broom and rested her double chin on the handle.

'Come in, young lad!' she said in a deep voice. 'I can see ye're just up from the country. Is it wid a drover ye travelled? Tell me his name and, if I know the chap, I'll find ye a corner to sleep in, even if tis under the stairs or behind the coal house! I'm the Widda MacNally and, because I'll never forget me poor husband, I have a kindness for all drovers. Speak up now! Who sent ye?'

'You're very good, ma'am!' said Shane. 'Only I don't want a lodging. I have one. I'm looking for a drover by the name of Tim Madden. He's me uncle and I'm up from Ballylicky.'

Mrs MacNally rolled up her sleeves, folded her short arms around the broom, and sighed.

'Ye'll not find him here, that's sure! There was a quare class of a chap up from the West, on his way to England. Desprit lonely, he was! The poor omadhaun had never left home before and he was petrified at the thought of all the misfortune before him.'

'Why was he going?' interrupted Shane, a bit scornfully.

'Why, is it? Because his married sister had sent for him! Why else? Had the job waiting and all! But the night he came here he was thinking he'd be wise to strike the trail back home!'

'Coward!' muttered Shane.

'I wouldn't say that!' declared Mrs MacNally, leaning comfortably on the broom. 'There's some do well across the seas. More wish they'd stayed in the place they knew. We were all sorry for the crathure! But up he went to the Cattle Market to see was there an odd drover or two from his own part, and if he didn't come back wid yer Uncle Tim Madden, lave it so! Tim, God be good to him, had been here before, so we gave him a grand welcome! He listened to the sorras of the chap from the West, did his best to cheer him up, and, when the time came, went off wid him to the North Wall, to see him safe on the boat for Liverpool!'

'What happened then?' cried Shane.

'What happened, is it? Sorra one o' me knows! No doubt the boyo from the West sailed away in the boat and, it might be, yer uncle went wid him! All I know is, he hasn't been back and his bits of things and his bag are up yonder waiting for him. What he owes me is nobody's business. Well I know if poor Tim Madden ever returns to Dublin, he'll settle up every penny piece!'

'Thank you, Mrs MacNally!' said Shane, going down the steps.

'Not so much hurry on ye!' exclaimed the big woman. 'Where's yerself staying?'

'At the Four Masters' Bookshop!' he told her proudly. 'Mrs Flanagan, there, told me she knew you!'

'Now why in the world didn't ye tell me that to begin wid? But I'm surprised that Mrs Flanagan, me own friend, never let on they were druv to take in lodgers! Ah well, a still tongue never broke a wumman's jaw yet! After all, what can they be doing, only pulling the devil be the tail! Sure, they don't sell a book from one year's end to the other! Poor as a church mouse, the bookseller is! That wife of his with her nose stuck in a book from morning till night!'

'I'm not a lodger!' said Shane, with great scorn in his voice.

'I'm the new shop boy! And why wouldn't Mrs O'Clery read books when they're all round her! You'd pick flowers if you had a garden, wouldn't you?'

Mrs MacNally laughed until she shook.

'Aren't ye the boyo! The O'Clerys will be made up now they've ye to mind the shop! Sell all the books ye can and don't let the corner boys of Dublin run off wid what they've no wish to read!'

'I won't!' promised Shane.

'And listen now! Why wouldn't ye go down to the North Wall one evening when the Liverpool boat is in and ask one of the sailors had he tidings of Tim Madden? Sure, there'd be no harm in that!'

'I will!' said Shane.

'Every night, bar Sunday, is the night when the boat goes out. Eight o'clock it starts! If ye get any news come back and tell me! I've a great liking for Tim Madden!'

As Shane went back to the shop on the quay he no longer felt a stranger in this big city. He had a job. He had a place to sleep in, better than he had ever had before. He had friends and all the books in the world to read. He picked up a stick and swished the air as if he were a drover. He swaggered a little too as he thought of all he'd have to tell Uncle Tim when they met again, and didn't even feel disappointed at not finding him.

The shop was as he had left it. The bookseller was still sitting on the step-ladder. Only now he nursed two volumes. Mrs O'Clery sat with her chin raised, her eyes dreamy, marking her place in the book with a knitting-needle, while a big ball of crimson wool lay on the floor at her feet.

It would be only manners to ask what he should do, thought Shane. But why disturb them?

'There's plenty work here!' he said to himself. 'Aunt Maureen would have every one of those books down and dusted.'

He went as far away as he could from the two readers. Here was a pile of old, dirty books. He drew his finger across the cover of the top one and brought away a thick coating of dust. Beneath was revealed dark green leather lined in gold.

'Must be precious!' decided Shane, and backed away.

He found himself against the bookshelves which lined the walls and turned carefully. So far he had done no harm.

'I could clean the windows! Then people would see the books properly. But first I'd have to shift them!'

He looked at Mrs O'Clery. She wasn't reading, only thinking. He picked up the ball of wool.

'Excuse me, ma'am!' he ventured. 'Would you want me to clean this window?'

She did not answer. He had seen Bridgie tugging her mother's sleeve to rouse her attention. But he didn't dare. He drifted to the door and out on the quay.

Shane looked at the piles of magazines and paper-covered books on the ledge at each side of the door. They were dumped, without arrangement, and he set himself to sort them out. He smoothed corners, put stories with stories, small magazines with their own kind, and big American picture journals in order.

Passers-by stopped, looked, and began to turn over the pages.

'Sixpence?' asked one man, picking up the best of the Americans and holding out a coin.

Shane took the money.

'Should know the right price!' he muttered.

He stared in at the bookseller and his wife. At the top of the stairs stretched Mog, her tail curled over her paws, her unwinking eyes fixed upon the door.

'Waiting for Bridgie!' decided the boy. 'I'll wait for Patrick. He might know!'

Shane leaned against the door-post, where the autumn sun shone full upon him. He had started making the doorway look decent. That was something. Wouldn't it be grand if he could make this shop a place where people would stand and look and buy and come again! Then the O'Clerys would be rich and they'd say how their luck had turned from the time Shane Madden from Ballylicky had stopped outside their shop to stare at the pictures in *Gulliver's Travels*. One day when he, Shane, was fixing the window so that it looked better than it had ever looked before, a drover with red hair and dancing blue eyes would go marching by on his way to the Cattle Market. He'd have a flock of sheep with him and they'd all come crowding on the pavement and, maybe, one or two would butt their way into the shop.

'If it isn't young Shane!' the drover would shout and he'd answer, 'If it isn't Uncle Tim!'

'Hallo, Shane!' said a voice. 'You've started work!'

There was Patrick – and Bridgie!

She had no greeting for him. She dashed past, up the stairs and dropped beside Mog, who stood on his hind legs, rubbed his head against Bridgie's chin, and purred so loudly Shane could hear him, and Patrick too.

The boys laughed. Mr O'Clery started and almost dropped his books. Mrs O'Clery looked round.

'The scholars are home!' sighed the bookseller.

'Was there any news at Mrs MacNally's?' asked Mrs O'Clery, smiling. 'It's time for tea! Tell us then!'

12. The Liverpool Boat

The O'Clerys were always most business-like at teatime. It was the meal they liked best, especially when Mrs Flanagan fried sausages, white pudding, and eggs. At breakfast the children were in a rush, dinner was an interruption, but at tea the long evening stretched before them.

'Here's your chair!' announced Bridgie, pushing Shane towards the seat beside her father's. 'Now you can tell us the whole story properly.'

Every one of the O'Clerys looked at him expectantly. Mrs Flanagan paused half-way between the kitchen and the table, the big hot dish of food held before her.

'Only if you wish!' added Mrs O'Clery.

She dropped her book on the table just inside the room and laid her knitting beside it. Mr O'Clery stuffed yet another volume at his back.

'It's not much of a story!' protested the boy, though now he was eager to tell it. 'You've heard most of it!'

'In bits and pieces!' declared Bridgie contemptuously. 'That's no way to tell a story!'

'Hark at the young madam!' cried Mrs Flanagan.

Shane ate slowly, telling, between bites, all he had left out. As he spoke, Ballylicky seemed far away, small and strange. He no longer felt his old dislike for Uncle Joseph. Aunt Maureen and the children were like people in a book. He had turned a page and they were almost forgotten.

'Uncle Tim was the one that mattered!' he said.

Mrs Flanagan set another slice of white pudding on his plate. It was crisp and savoury. Yet he sat looking at it without relish.

'He was the one you could count on!' he said.

'Yet he was the one that went away unbeknownst!' the widow told him, blowing her cup full of hot tea.

Shane scowled at her.

'You never knew him!' he declared.

'Now! Now! Sourpuss!' she retorted.

Mr O'Clery was steadily eating his fried egg, his sausage, and the thick pieces of white pudding. He didn't like white pudding. He hated black pudding. He wished Mrs Flanagan would give him two eggs instead. He didn't want to ask her. It might hurt her feelings.

'Why don't you give dadda two fried eggs?' demanded Bridgie, looking up at her. 'Then he could give his white pudding to Mog. Poor Mog never has enough white pudding. I only leave him the skins!'

'Isn't she the lassie?' demanded Mrs Flanagan, looking round with a delighted grin. 'Would ye care for another egg, Mr O'Clery?'

'It would make a change!' he told her.

She slapped down her knife and fork, and marched cheerfully into the kitchen.

'How did you guess?' Mr O'Clery asked his daughter.

'I just thought!' she answered.

They smiled triumphantly at one another.

'I wonder where your uncle has gone?' said Mrs O'Clery to Shane. 'Mrs MacNally is right! You should go down to the North Wall.'

'What would be the use of that, Eilis?' asked her husband. 'Who would remember one man out of so many?'

'They'd remember Uncle Tim!' declared Shane proudly. 'They always do! I'll go tonight!'

'I'll come with you!' Patrick told him.

'So will I!' put in Bridgie.

'How about your home lessons?' asked their mother. 'If Shane has no news tonight and wants to go on Saturday, you can go then.'

So Shane went alone. It was a straight line along the dark quays, past the glittering lights around O'Connell Bridge, beyond Butt Bridge and the Customs House. Here men, with mongrel dogs and bulging sacks, sprawled on the wide steps. Some were playing cards. Others gazed out on the river and the ships anchored there, like men in a dream. One, a large garden fork across his knees, smoked a pipe comfortably and followed the passers-by with his quick, smiling eyes. His clothes were worn. He had a thick muffler round his neck and his shoes were sound. The other men were ragged. One had red toes poking through split boots.

The space behind the grand pillars sheltered them, but Shane knew how hard and cold stones grew at night.

'If it wasn't for the O'Clerys, I'd be like them!' thought the boy sympathetically.

On Rogerson's Quay, at the other side of the river, the cranes were still. Two little girls were dancing on the cobbles and a crowd watched their clever steps.

At first Shane walked quickly. But the nearer he came to the sheds where he could see big passenger steamers moored close in, the slower he went.

He passed one low down in the water. She looked very clean and proud, with her cream coat and the name *Lady Gwendoline* picked out in blue and brown. At the stern fluttered a blue flag with a golden harp and, on a lifebelt, hanging by the bridge, 'Liverpool' was printed round it in thick black letters.

'If they tell me Uncle Tim went away on a boat, should I follow him?' thought the boy. 'But how can I? Maybe I should wait! When I have the fare, I can make up me mind. All I have now is the shilling Mrs Flanagan lent me.'

Men, cases on their shoulders, trudged along the gutter. Girls, in twos and threes, carrying parcels and bags, hurried by, their high heels tapping. Taxis and lorries streamed along the roadway. Puddles gleamed. Straws and crumpled paper scurried before the wind. Overhead the lights shone steadily. Higher still, stars glittered in the dark sky. Men stumbled out from eating and drinking shops. Groups gathered at corners. Cries of 'Good-bye now!' 'We'll see you to the boat!' 'Don't forget your old friends!' 'Come back with a fortune!' 'Mind you write a long letter every week!' were tossed along the quays. Hootings and shouts and splashings rose from the river and the air throbbed.

Now the high gloomy sheds rose, shutting out all sight of the ships. Between them were iron railings, with closed gates and Shane could hear the water lapping against the quay walls.

'Is this the way for the Liverpool boat that's going off to-night?' he asked every loiterer he passed. Not because he doubted it but because he wanted to hear the answer, 'Why wouldn't it be?' or 'Doesn't everyone know this is the place for the Liverpool boat?' 'Haven't ye two eyes in yer head? If ye can't see the ship itself by raison of the old sheds blocking the view, isn't that the Liverpool Bar over yonder? Up in the red lights! That tells ye!'

In the high wall were two narrow doors and here the passengers showed their tickets. Shane squeezed close to the man in charge at the steerage entrance.

'Do you be here every night when the Liverpool boat is going out?' asked Shane.

'I do indeed!' replied the man. 'If not me, then another! There's always one of us to guard the Liverpool boat.'

'Do you remember Tim Madden coming here? He's me uncle, a drover from West Cork.'

'That's a tough question, lad!' declared the man, never ceasing to look at tickets. 'A very tough question! There's only hundreds and hundreds raging along here night after night, with friends and neighbours, not to mention relations, come to see the last of them. That's all! And ye expect me to remember a West Cork drover! Haven't I something better to be doing with me time and me interest?'

'He's tall and thin!' persisted Shane. 'He has red hair and blue eyes. He can sing and whistle better than anyone else and he's the finest drover in all Cork. He can do anything with animals!'

'So that's his name, is it!' cried the man indignantly. 'Tim Madden, the impudent scoundrel! Well I remember him, and if I see him again I'll have a few words with that same boyo! When ye find him, ye can tell him I'm here, waiting!'

'Did he go away on the boat?' asked Shane, pressing close to the fence, for passengers and their luggage were crowding through.

'If I knew that, I'd be wiser than I am!' said the man bitterly. 'It was the busiest night of the year and, before I

He reached O'Connell Bridge. The gay lights of O'Connell Street gleamed with a gentle shimmer through the rain. Beyond, lines of silver lights reached into the darkness.

'Dublin's a grand city,' he thought. 'It's almost as good as Cork!'

He crossed to Bachelors' Walk with the crowd, trying not to show his dread of the great buses, the stream of motors, the cyclists darting from unexpected directions like wasps.

There were fewer people here, so he began to run, and came upon the bookshop before he expected it.

The outside books had been taken away but there were customers inside the lighted shop.

'Isn't it well for Mr O'Clery he has me now!' thought the boy. 'How will I begin?'

He put his cap and coat behind the door and went over to a man holding a book and staring hopelessly about.

'Can I help you, sir?' he asked.

He had served three people when Mr O'Clery looked out, saw Shane, and went on mending the spine of a heavy, leather-bound volume.

When the customers were gone, Shane put the money he had taken in the drawer of the desk in the corner behind a rampart of huge books and stood looking into the big room. Mrs Flanagan's chair was drawn up to the fire. The O'Clerys sat round the table, bending over their tasks. He smiled as he watched them. He could go in and be welcomed. They'd want to know what had happened.

Bridgie looked up.

'Here's Shane back home!' she cried.

Then he stepped through the doorway.

could stop him, a redheaded lad that might be your uncle, for the other chap was calling him "his darling Tim", dashed through and nearly flattened me. I saw one ticket and one ticket only! Sure they wouldn't let him on board without one, and if they did, he wouldn't be let land the other side!'

'Did you see him again?' asked Shane.

'I did not and, what's more, I don't want to! Off with you now! If I set eyes on that long, lanky drover again, he'll not pass me if he has twenty tickets! If you want to see the *Munster* going down the river, get along there!'

A sudden piercing blast sent Shane running. He had imagined he would see emigrants swarming up crowded gangways and the ship sinking lower and lower as each one stepped on deck, but the high shed had hidden all that.

He followed others hurrying over a narrow bridge and out on to an open part of the quay. Now he could see the *Munster*, a light low down on its mast, a huge funnel, and rows of white faces turned towards the crowd. He listened to the cries of farewell, the promises to write, the good wishes. The sounds were confused. If Uncle Tim had been there, his voice would have been caught up in the general tumult, his face a white oval.

The ship was moving slowly past them. Now it swung out to the centre of the river. The rows of faces were hidden by a forest of waving hands and handkerchiefs. Shane pulled off his scarf and waved that. The lights were growing dimmer until only the red stern light could be seen as the boat steamed out into Dublin Bay.

Shane felt he was saying a long good-bye to Uncle Tim.

'Even if he hadn't a ticket, they might be easy on him!' thought the boy. 'No one but Uncle Joseph ever stood out against Tim Madden!'

The drizzle was turning to a downpour. There was no shelter unless he stood in a doorway, and Shane was longing to be back in the Four Masters' Bookshop.

13. The Ice Maiden

'He's back! Shane's back!' cried Bridgie, flinging down her pen and jumping up from the table.

She caught the boy's hand and pulled him in to the comfort of the room.

'Where's your Uncle Tim? Where is he? Did you find him?'

The others looked up from their tasks. Shane saw the interest and friendliness in their eyes.

'Uncle Tim was at the North Wall one night with another man! The ticket man told me that. There was a great crowd and he couldn't be sure if me uncle went away on the boat.'

Mr O'Clery was wrapping a parcel of books. Mrs O'Clery had stopped reading to listen but she went on with her knitting.

'You could call at Mrs MacNally's any time you're near the Cattle Market,' said the bookseller. 'She knows you're here, so if your uncle didn't go on the boat, he'll most likely call to her and she'll tell him where you are. If he did go to Liverpool, you'll just have to wait till he comes back. Are you good at tying knots?'

Shane tied the knots securely. He knew few could best him at that.

Mrs O'Clery reached out and touched his coat.

'That's damp!' she said. 'Patrick! Will you lend Shane your best jacket while his is drying? This should be hanging on the kitchen door. Hurry now! You don't want the lad to be sneezing and coughing all night!'

Without a word, Patrick ran upstairs and came back with his navy blue jacket over his arm. Shane's fingers fumbled at the buttons for they were stiff with cold and he was confused at so much kindness.

'You'll need another suit!' Mrs O'Clery told him. 'And a raincoat!'

'He can have my mack until he gets his own!' offered Patrick. 'It might be a bit tight.'

'I'll alter the buttons,' said his mother. 'Bring it down, there's the boy!'

'You're terribly good!' murmured Shane, as he snuggled his shoulders into the warm dry coat. 'And you hardly know me!'

'Every day will alter that!' Mr O'Clery told him, as he began sorting a pile of books. 'Soon we'll wonder how we ever managed without you. Look! Mark these sixpence and these a shilling. I'll think about the rest. Unless you're tired?'

'I'm never tired!' boasted Shane. 'It's lucky for me you needed a boy!'

He looked round doubtfully. 'You did need a boy, didn't you?'

Patrick pulled a sheet of cardboard from a shelf and held it up.

'Look at this! I did it a month ago. Dad puts it in the window and takes it out again.'

Shane read – *Shop Boy Wanted. Must Be Good At Reading Writing, Arithmetic.*

The words were printed by hand and Shane had never seen such printing. The capitals had tiny pictures inside each curve. All the letters had flourishes, yet the notice was so distinct it could be read yards away.

'I copied the big letters from the Book of Kells, up in Trinity College,' said Patrick. 'It's the best printing I've done. But the pictures should be coloured.'

'I'm lucky you wanted a boy!' said Shane thankfully.

'We're lucky too!' Mrs O'Clery told him kindly. 'We didn't want any boy!'

She went on with her reading and knitting. Patrick and Bridgie toiled at their homework.

'Now I'm going to work here, I should know what to do,' said Shane. 'I must know all about books!'

Mr O'Clery put his hand on the boy's shoulder and led him back to the shop.

'I've been at this job for a lifetime,' he said. 'Still, I don't know all about books. You'll begin at the beginning. Keep those on the shelves dusted and tidy. The piles I put on the floor you can arrange outside, every morning. As for the others, I mark the price inside the cover – when I remember. Clean the window when you can. Sweep the floor every day. Mrs Flanagan washes it once a week. Watch out for customers and don't read more than you can help while you're supposed to be working. It's a habit. It grows on you! You'll learn the rest as we go along!'

'What time do we open the shop?' asked Shane.

'Nine is early enough. We should close at six. Often I forget and many a time I've sold more books in an evening after six than during the rest of the week. People who buy books are free then. And Shane, if anyone reads without buying, take no notice!'

Mr O'Clery picked up a book and began to turn the pages.

'How many cows did you have in the country?' called Bridgie from the room.

'Six!' answered Shane, going in to her.

'Could you milk them?'

The boy was indignant.

'Of course I could! I can do everything on a farm, almost everything.'

Bridgie had her rag doll on her lap. The cat sat beside her. Her school books were scattered over the table. She pushed her silky black hair back, put her elbows on the table, and gazed up at Shane.

'How many cousins have you?' she asked.

'Four!'

'Are they all girls or all boys?'

'Two of each!'

'It isn't mannerly to ask so many questions!' said Mrs O'Clery.

But she was listening too.

'If he'd tell me properly, I wouldn't have to ask!' complained Bridgie.

'Shane! We'll close now!' called Mr O'Clery from the shop.

He showed the boy how to fix the bar across the door and draw the shutters, so that the books in the window were still on view.

'Now your time is your own, to read, to study, visit the city, or do anything that interests you,' said the bookseller. 'I hope you'll be happy with us.'

'Mr O'Clery!' said the boy. 'Could I have that book to read, the one that was in the window, *Gulliver's Travels*? I didn't have a chance to finish the one Uncle Tim bought me.'

'You can – if Bridgie will allow you,' said the bookseller, laughing.

'Bridgie!' he called. 'Will you share *Gulliver's Travels* with Shane?'

She came out to them, the cat marching beside her, the rag doll under her arm. Shane wondered why her mother or father didn't buy her a proper doll.

'I'll save up and buy her a beauty for Christmas!' he decided, feeling rich already now that he was going to earn money.

'If I let you have Gulliver now, promise you'll give it back when I'm going up to bed,' she bargained.

'I promise!' he said cheerfully.

'Suppose Shane wants to read in bed,' said her father. 'You wouldn't begrudge him that, would you?'

'No!' she agreed. 'I wouldn't grudge that to the poor boy. I have Mog and Migeen!'

Mr O'Clery laughed. But Shane looked at her seriously.

'Thanks!' he said. 'I'll take great care of the book.'

'When you've finished, you can tell me the story,' Bridgie told him. 'Then we'll put the book back in the window.'

'You're very lazy, Bridgie!' said Mrs O'Clery as they came back to the fire. 'Patrick spoils you, telling stories when you should read them yourself – a great girl of ten!'

'Ten's not all that old!' cried Bridgie. 'Anyway I'm the youngest here, except Mog and Migeen! Shane! How old is your cousin Maggie?'

'Nine!' replied the boy.

'She's younger than I am!' said the child. 'I expect she misses you a lot. I'll bring you down the book! I'll let you keep it, even if you don't tell me every bit!'

They made room for Shane and the big volume at the table. He had never known such comfort. The soft, shaded light, the fire of turf and logs, the pleasant smell and puffing of Mr O'Clery's pipe, came between him and the strange story of dwarfs, giants, and talking horses which, he knew, meant more than the adventures that were told.

'Do you like blue, or would you prefer green?' Mrs O'Clery asked him, holding up a skein of wool in each hand.

'Grey, to match his eyes!' interrupted Bridgie.

'You'll need a warm jersey for the winter!' explained Mrs O'Clery. 'We all wear jerseys!'

'You're terribly good, ma'am!' blurted Shane. 'But you shouldn't, really you shouldn't!'

Mrs O'Clery laughed at him.

'You can't be the only one in the family without a jersey,' she said. 'You wouldn't want to disgrace me?'

He shook his head. He couldn't speak.

Quickly Shane fitted into the life at the bookshop. While Patrick lay dreaming, the boy from Ballylicky was out on the quayside, cleaning the windows, sweeping the pavement, running to the river wall to hail the swans, gazing at the sea-gulls and envying them as they hung motionless in the air, then, curving sideways, soared by the golden angel opposite, high above the sleeping city.

He watched the sun rise over Dublin Bay and turned to see the towers of Christ Church and the spires of St Patrick's emerge from the river mists, to stand guardian over the huddle of houses in the Liberties and the Coombe.

Uncle Tim had said Shane would like Dublin. Already he loved it. Everyone else was tired of Bridgie's enthusiasm for exploring. But Shane was ready to go down any turning, make for any tree or building seen in the distance, and wander across the great stretches of the Phoenix Park. He was even willing to carry Migeen buttoned under his coat.

He played hurley with Patrick and his friends in the park and learned to ride the old bicycle. He determined to go every Wednesday morning to the Cattle Market. But when the morning arrived he felt it would be foolish.

If Tim came to Dublin, he would hear of his nephew at Mrs MacNally's and, if he had gone to Liverpool, there would be no trace of him at the market, or Stoney Batter either. After a few Wednesdays he forgot and only wondered about his uncle when a man jumped into the Liffey to rescue a child or a lad stopped a runaway bullock.

'That's just what Uncle Tim would do!' he declared proudly.

'Mebbe he would and mebbe he wouldn't!' said Mrs Flanagan.

'Tell me more about Uncle Tim!' ordered Bridgie.

Shane was willing but he did not realize that he was no longer telling the truth about life at the farm. He recalled only Aunt Maureen's kindness, the fun he had with the children, the sweet blackberries and huge mushrooms, the bags of nuts for Hallowe'en. He forgot the hardness of life on the Cork farm. One day he would go back there, loaded with toys and sweets – when Uncle Tim returned to Dublin.

He seldom spoke of Uncle Joseph, but he told more and more of Uncle Tim's courage, Uncle Tim's generosity, his adventures, the wonderful stories he told in bed at night, and the great things he promised.

The better Shane came to know Dublin, the more dream-like his old life seemed.

On Saturday mornings a man with a cap pulled over his eyes stood at the corner and sang 'In Dublin's Fair City where the girls are so pretty', 'Mrs Mulligan the Pride of the Coombe', and the song of the mariners on one of the Guinness barges:

> *'As we go down the Liffey*
> *All the bowsies on the quay,*
> *Shout "Bring us back a parrot*
> *When ye come home from say!"'*

The singer never asked for money but Mrs O'Clery always sent Bridgie over to him with a sixpenny piece. He would ask Bridgie which songs she would wish him to sing next time he came. But whatever she asked for, they were the three he always sang.

'Mebbe the poor man doesn't know any others,' Mrs Flanagan told the little girl, when she complained.

There was the thin, brown-faced woman who came from the vegetable market with cauliflowers, cabbages, carrots, tomatoes, and oranges in a big square basket on wheels. Her baby, wrapped in a ragged shawl, was perched against the handles and, while Mrs Flanagan picked out the vegetables they needed, the woman sat on the step and drank a cup of tea; the baby chewed a cut of bread and jam.

The second time Shane saw her she stared at him, then at the shop.

'So ye're the shop boy there's all the talk about?' she asked.

'I am!' he told her proudly.

'So I suppose tis ye're to blame for the stark, bare, clane look of the place?'

He did not answer, but Mrs O'Clery, dropping the book she had just taken from the shelf, walked across the shop and put her hand on the boy's shoulder.

'He's responsible for it all, Mary!' she said. 'He's the shop boy we've been wanting for years!'

Mary finished her tea and turned the cup upside down on the saucer.

'The Widda Flanagan makes good tay!' she declared. 'But she don't lave a poor wumman a scrap of luck, good or bad, in it! Are ye from the Black North, young lad?'

'I come from Ballylicky in West Cork!' Shane answered crossly.

'No insult intended, ye young curmudgeon! That'll be two shillings, Mrs Flanagan! The cauliflower and the oranges alone is worth every penny of it. Me man will bring the sack of praties when he comes from the job.'

She wrapped her shawl tighter about her, settled the baby more comfortably, and strode off along the quay, pushing the wheeled basket with one hand, gripping her shawl together with the other.

Bridgie was standing in the doorway, looking out, the rag doll under her arm.

'Look, Shane!' she whispered. 'There's Imelda Deasy from round the corner, with her new doll and pram! Isn't she lovely?'

A tall, slender child, dressed in blue, with golden hair falling over her shoulders, walked beside the river wall, wheeling a doll's pram. It was very grand and everyone passing along turned to look at her.

'Friend of yours?' asked Shane.

'I wouldn't dare talk to her!' confessed Bridgie. 'She goes to the Convent over beyond Stephen's Green and she plays the piano. I'd sooner be friends with her than with any other girl in the world!'

'The stiff, cocked-up young madam!' snorted Mrs Flanagan, beating a batter pudding with great vigour as she looked out on the quay over Bridgie's head. 'Sure, ye have no sense, Bridgie!'

99

'We call her the Ice Maiden!' laughed Mrs O'Clery. 'Her father is a very clever solicitor and she's an only child. She is a lovely little thing! But I'm afraid she's terribly conceited!'

'Why shouldn't she be?' cried Bridgie. 'She's like a fairy princess!'

'Go over and show her Migeen!' suggested Patrick mischievously. 'I know she's never seen a doll to equal yours!'

Bridgie scowled. Her face flushed. She flung up her head.

'Migeen mayn't be beautiful!' she said. 'But she's not an ordinary doll!'

She ran out on the pavement. For a moment the roadway was empty and she darted across. Mog followed as far as the kerb and sat there looking after her gravely.

As Bridgie came up with Imelda, she wished she was back in the shop. But the boys were watching and pride forced her on.

There were two dolls in the pram. Both were dressed in blue and looked as grand as their young mistress.

'What a lovely pram!' said Bridgie desperately. 'I never had two dolls at the one time. Is it your birthday?'

Imelda looked sideways at her but did not answer.

'This is my doll, Migeen!' and Bridgie held out the rag doll.

Mrs Flanagan had made the rag doll to amuse Bridgie when she was sick with a bad cold. The arms and legs were rolled-up dusters, the soft body was an old towel. The head was a flour bag stuffed with ends of wool. Patrick had painted the face and it was strangely alive. Mrs O'Clery had knitted its clothes and Bridgie felt proud of them.

She looked beseechingly at Imelda. If they could admire one another's dolls, one day they might be friends.

Imelda glanced at the smaller girl with an indignant frown.

'Take away your ugly dirty old doll! Don't you dare let it touch mine!'

She thrust out her hand and sent Migeen flying over the low wall into the river.

Startled at what she had done, Imelda ran along the quay, pushing the pram before her.

Bridgie, even more startled, leaned over the wall and saw Migeen, on her back, drifting with the current.

'Look!' she called to a man standing up in a boat, which he was rowing towards O'Connell Bridge.

'Bless and save us!' exclaimed the man. 'There's a child in the river and me not able to swim a stroke!'

Not sure what was happening, Patrick raced across the road, dodging among motors, carts, and lorries. Shane kept beside him.

'What's happened?' he asked, as they reached Bridgie. 'Is it the doll? Did the other young one toss it in the river?'

He wasn't much troubled. It was a shame for Bridgie to have only that makeshift of a doll. Patrick's concern astonished him. If it had been the cat now!

'We'll get Migeen back!' promised Patrick. 'Come down the steps, Shane! Wish we had a stick!'

Bridgie was before them, running her hardest, so that she reached the narrow stone steps leading to the water as the man in the boat drew in to the quayside. Bridgie, standing on tiptoe, was preparing to jump aboard. Patrick grabbed her frock and pulled her back. But Shane, as the boat almost touched the wall, put his hand on the man's shoulder and stepped in.

'If you'd row out,' he said, 'I'll catch it easy with your boathook. Look! There it goes!'

The man stared and laughed.

'Thanks be! I thought 'twas a child! Is it a dolly?'

'It is! Quick now, before it gets too far!' pleaded the boy.

'Aren't ye young ones great for giving orders!' chuckled the boatman. 'Ah well, I've chisellers of me own!'

With powerful strokes he urged the boat under O'Connell Bridge, where a row of faces gazed down upon them.

'Is the child safe?' called an anxious voice.

'Safe and sound!' shouted back the oarsman with a grin.

As they came to the other side of the bridge, Shane caught Migeen with the boat-hook and pulled her in.

'That's a queer class of a doll!' exclaimed the man. 'I've seen young Bridgie with it many a time.'

'I'm going to save up to buy her a proper one!' Shane told him.

The man nodded.

'Good lad! Good lad! But I'm telling ye! Little Bridgie loves that bundle of rags! She mightn't be so set on a grand new one. She's not like that young madam that careers up and down as if she was the Queen of Sheba. Sit down now! I'm turning the boat and I'm not wishing to pull yerself out of the Liffey with the old boat-hook. One rescue a day is enough for any man!'

14. The Lost Puppet

'You have Migeen safe?' asked Patrick eagerly, as Shane landed on the steps and the boatman rowed leisurely upstream, smiling as he thought of the rag doll and Bridgie.

'The poor little chiseller!' he muttered. 'Her heart's broke over that bundle of wet rags!'

Shane put the limp doll into Bridgie's hands.

'She'll be grand once she's dry!' he said comfortingly.

He remembered how Maggie had cried when Jer flung her doll at Des. It fell on the earthen floor and the wax face broke in three. Aunt Maureen stuck the pieces together and Maggie was happy again.

But looking at Bridgie's solemn face he knew that Migeen would never be the same to her. The doll's hair was gone, the face a dirty smudge, the arms and legs coated with brown mud.

'I'll buy you a new one!' he told her. 'One with golden hair and blue eyes. I'll start saving up this week.'

'I hate golden hair and blue eyes!' snapped Bridgie.

They waited for a gap in the traffic, then crossed to the bookshop. Mr O'Clery was arranging books and didn't notice them as they went through.

'Poor Migeen!' said Mrs O'Clery, who was mending torn pages at the desk. 'What can I do for her?'

Bridgie sniffed. Her mother laid down the paste brush and put her arms round her.

'Don't take it too hard!' she said. 'We'll buy you a grand, new doll.'

'She wasn't an ugly, dirty, old doll!' wailed Bridgie, while Mrs O'Clery wiped her tears away. 'She was Migeen, and now she isn't anything any more!'

'I could shake that Imelda, the consated little image!' declared Mrs Flanagan, coming over with a hot sausage-roll. 'Put yerself outside this and take comfort. I'll dry Migeen and yer mammy will knit her new clothes. Patrick will draw her face fine and strong, and she'll be as good as ever!'

Bridgie slowly ate the hot sausage-roll. It was comforting, but the wet bundle on her lap reproached her.

'I only wanted to be friends!' she said mournfully.

'Look!' whispered her mother. 'You've never seen dolls like those before.'

A tall girl with dark, curling hair was standing with Mr O'Clery in the shop. She had settled a long basket between them and, as they watched, she put in her hand and lifted something out. Mr O'Clery laughed.

'Now isn't that very strange!' he said. 'Bridgie! Here are dolls of a kind you've never seen!'

'If that isn't mighty like a leprechaun!' cried Mrs Flanagan.

Bridgie went slowly into the shop.

The strange girl was holding up a little man in green, wearing a leather apron and a long, tasselled cap. He had a grey beard and, though his face was cross and wrinkled, he danced up and down on the floor.

Bridgie ran over. The stranger looked down at her with a friendly smile, then she saw the rag doll, wet and stained with the river mud.

'Show me!' she said.

Bridgie held up Migeen.

'She was thrown in the river!' the little girl explained.

'The poor doll!' exclaimed the stranger. 'Now what can we do about her?'

Bending over her basket, she picked out a little woman with a black shawl, a red skirt, and a check apron.

Bridgie edged closer and saw that the basket was filled with a strange collection of animals and dolls.

'These are puppets!' the girl told her. 'They're more alive than dolls. They can do wonders! But you must help them.'

'Migeen isn't an ordinary doll!' protested Bridgie. 'I'd sooner have her than the best doll in the world. But she's spoilt now!'

'Would you like one of these to make up?' asked the stranger.

Bridgie shook her head.

'Would you let me try to make your doll better? Suppose I turned her into a puppet?'

Bridgie stared from the rag doll to the basketful of puppets, then slowly held out Migeen.

Patrick looked over his sister's head.

'I've seen those puppets!' he said. 'They talk and dance and sing! If you could turn Migeen into one it would be grand!'

He felt guilty. If he hadn't encouraged Bridgie to show her doll to Imelda there would have been no trouble at all.

'Shall I take your poor Migeen away and turn her into a puppet?'

The girl put her head on one side inquiringly.

'Please!' said Bridgie.

'When it's finished, maybe Mrs Flanagan will bring it along?'

'Indeed I will, love!' declared the widow. 'The sooner the better!'

'Now I'll take my book!' said the girl.

'It's in with the puppets!' Mr O'Clery told her. 'And any book you ever want from the shop is yours!'

The girl smiled at them all and went down the quay, her basket on her arm.

'You won't forget Migeen?' Bridgie asked anxiously.

'Deed then and I won't!' replied the widow.

Each morning Bridgie ran to meet Mrs Flanagan as she came in with the shopping.

'Show me!' she cried. 'Show me!'

'I will when the time comes!' was the answer.

On the seventh morning, Bridgie was helping Shane to arrange the books and magazines outside the shop when she saw Mrs Flanagan coming down the quay. She walked sideways because of the heavy market bag. The wind tugged at her coat, which was always unbuttoned, and a lock of her grey hair tossed above her head like a plume.

She walked quickly and, even at that distance, Bridgie could see her trying to hold her lips firm and not come along smiling.

'She's got Migeen!' cried Bridgie.

Bridgie started to run. Shane held her back.

'Mrs Flanagan won't utter until she's inside the shop!' he declared.

Bridgie knew he was right. So she waited.

But she could call and she did, putting her hands to her mouth.

'You have Migeen?'

Mrs Flanagan nodded. Bridgie shook herself free of Shane and raced along the quay, her hair blown back from her face.

'Is she lovely?' she asked, dancing up and down excitedly.

'She is so, God bless you! Lovelier than ever poor Migeen was!'

Bridgie stopped, then ran to catch up.

'Isn't she like Migeen?'

'She is like Migeen! The exact same as Migeen, only better! You'll see! She's dressed in red, with a black shawl on her!'

'Wish I didn't have to go to school today!' sighed Bridgie as they came to the shop.

Mr O'Clery was opening a parcel the postman had just brought. Mrs O'Clery was standing before a shelf of books, wondering which she should read after breakfast. Patrick was coaxing Mog to jump over his joined hands. They all swung round.

'You have it!' cried Patrick. 'I can tell by the look in your eyes, Mrs Flanagan! That's grand!'

'Now we'll have our Bridgie back again instead of a little lost stranger!' said her father.

'Put the bag on the table!' advised Mrs O'Clery.

Shane came in from the shop. He loved watching Mrs Flanagan empty her market bag. So did they all.

She peered into the bag and looked puzzled.

'Isn't that very queer now! Sure, the crathure must have slipped down!'

Bridgie stood on tiptoe. Eyes wide open, lips apart, she sighed deeply.

Mrs Flanagan brought out the packet of tea from Lipton's and a blue paper bag of sugar. There was cornflour and a tin of unsweetened milk for making sauce. A cardboard box with a dozen eggs, securely stored, each in its little square nest, a two-pound jar of strawberry jam, a packet of cocoa, a packet of dried marrowfat peas, a lump of soft yellow cheese, a bag of mixed biscuits, a string of sausages, and a pound of minced beef escaping from its damp paper wrappings.

'Why did you put poor Migeen under all those things?' asked Bridgie reproachfully.

'Ah, child! Why would I be doing that?' cried Mrs Flanagan. 'I put the poor doll safe and snug right at the top, in between the tea and the cornflour. I thought she might have slipped down with me hurrying. But how could she? There's the bottom of the bag and she's not there!'

'You've lost her!' cried Bridgie. 'You've lost my Migeen!'

'God bless me soul!' exclaimed the widow. 'I was as careful as could be! She was in the bag just before ye let a roar out of ye! I'm dead sure of that!'

Mrs O'Clery pushed Bridgie towards the door.

'Run back the way Mrs Flanagan came and look in the gutter, look in the doorways and up the steps!'

Bridgie darted from the shop, Patrick with her. Shane stayed where he was.

Mrs Flanagan carried her shopping into the kitchen.

'I wouldn't have had this happen for worlds!' she lamented. 'There do be times when I wish I'd never made the old doll. I did it to give her a rise when she was sick, and she loved the crathure! And now she'll never forgive me! I know that one!'

Shane could see Patrick stooping to the gutters, running up the steps, bumping into men and women hurrying to offices, shops, and the market. Children, with heavy school bags on their backs, searched too, wondering what lost treasure the boy was seeking.

Bridgie ran before her brother for a while, then stood in the centre of the pavement, her head hanging down. A woman spoke to her, but Bridgie couldn't answer, and Patrick, realizing they had come far enough, put his arm round her and drew her back to the shop.

'Time for school,' said Mr O'Clery. 'You've trouble enough without being late!'

To everyone's surprise, Bridgie picked her bag up at once and went off meekly with Patrick.

'Wish I had the money now to buy her a proper doll!' thought Shane. 'But would it make up, I wonder?'

'Where is that *Grimms' Fairy Tales*?' asked Mrs O'Clery. 'They'd take Bridgie's mind off her loss.'

'On the top shelf in the corner,' the bookseller told her.

'Though I don't think they'll make any difference. Shane! Get the ladder! Look, that big book along there! No! No! No! Right in the corner!'

Shane found the book – big and heavy, a proper book, with a green-and-gold cover, and a picture to every other page. He began to read *The Three Ragamuffins*. He read on and on, turning the pages breathlessly, forgetting the shop, Bridgie, and her rag doll.

A customer, finding the bookseller absorbed in studying the torn title-page of a rare book and Mrs O'Clery too busy mending the worn corners of a volume of poetry to hear him, shook the ladder and startled the boy into attention.

'Do you want to sell books? Or is it a private library the boss is keeping?' demanded the man. 'I want a book to read on the train to Belfast and I've no time to waste!'

Shane scrambled down the ladder, still clutching *Grimms' Household Stories*.

'Take this!' he told the man. 'These stories are wonderful!'

The man took the book and held it at arm's length.

'Aren't they fairy stories?' he exclaimed. 'Am I a child?'

'I've read up to there!' Shane told him, showing a page half-way through the book. 'I haven't come across a single fairy! If you don't read this book, you'll be sorry all the days of your life! I wish this was my shop! I wouldn't let you have the book! I'd keep it to read myself. But I'm only the boy and it's my duty to sell the books!'

'Ah well!' sighed the traveller. 'If I don't like it I can bring it back when I'm in Dublin again. It's a mercy there's someone here who knows what a shop is for! How much? Five and six! Here you are!'

Snatching up his bag, he poked the book under his arm and hurried off.

Mr O'Clery looked up from the book he was studying.

'You're a good salesman, Shane. I hope that chap does like the book!'

Shane stared. So the bookseller had been listening.

'Would there be another book like that?' he asked wistfully. 'I didn't have time to read all the stories and I'd forgotten they were meant to comfort Bridgie!'

'There's another copy in the box yonder. But don't open it until the shop is shut!'

15. The Signature of Jonathan Swift

After dinner Shane was packing parcels of books to be sent to America. They had all been very silent. Bridgie's puzzled little face and downcast eyes made the others long to comfort her. But even Patrick found it difficult. Mrs O'Clery did try.

'We'll go to the toyshop in Mary Street and find a doll there!' she promised.

'Don't want a doll! Want Migeen!' murmured Bridgie, not even raising her eyes.

She went off to school with Patrick, not caring if she went or stayed.

'I should have bought her a doll on her birthday!' sighed Mrs O'Clery. 'Then she wouldn't have bothered about Migeen. But she seemed so sure she didn't want one.'

'I'll buy her one this Christmas!' Shane whispered to himself. 'And I'll buy presents for them all at Uncle Joseph's.'

On the widow's advice, Mr O'Clery had decided to give the boy ten shillings a week as well as his board and lodging. They had planned that he must have new boots, woollen underclothes, and a mackintosh. He could pay them back at half a crown a week. Then his money would be all his own.

Shane felt rich. But he wanted to send some money to Aunt Maureen. He wrote each Sunday and, though not one of his letters had been answered, he did not mind. He had never seen a letter written at the farm.

'You should ask your Cousin Maggie to write,' Mrs O'Clery told him.

'Sure, she's only a little girl, younger than Bridgie!' he declared.

'Bridgie can write a very good letter!' said Mrs O'Clery proudly. 'Patrick taught her when she was only six. They used to pass letters to one another across the table.'

There weren't many customers and Shane ventured to bring out the big *Gulliver's Travels* and open it on the table.

Mrs O'Clery smiled approvingly and settled to her own book.

As Shane turned the pages, a sheet of thick, yellowed paper dropped out. The boy picked it up and saw a familiar name written on it in queer crabbed letters:

> I promise to pay to *mrs* Martha Whiteway for the use of her Son John Whiteway, whenever he becomes to some able Chirurgian a Prentice,
>
> the Sum of one hundred pounds sterl,
>
> Witness
> my hand and Seal this fifteenth Day of May 1736 — six
>
> Jonath: Swift

This letter and signature is a facsimile of an actual letter by Jonathan Swift.

Someone had used the letter as a bookmark. He looked up to ask about it. But Mrs O'Clery was absorbed in her book, though her fingers knitted away as if they had a life of their own.

'I'll wait until Mr O'Clery is here. He'll know!' decided Shane.

He was still gazing at the discoloured paper and the crabbed writing when Patrick and Bridgie came in, cold and silent. Instead of running they had walked and they stood warming their hands at the fire.

'An end of this nonsense!' said Mrs Flanagan firmly, as she came in with the big teapot. 'I'll be seeing that Migeen in me dreams if this goes on. Take off them coats, the pair of ye, and sit up to the table. Have sense, Bridgie, or ye'll have us all as miserable as yerself! Look at poor Mog! The crathure doesn't know what's happening at all!'

Bridgie pulled off her coat and hugged the cat. Shane closed the letter in the book and put it back carefully in the window. As Mrs O'Clery came to the table, the bookseller entered.

He was humming cheerfully, and even Shane knew he had bought another treasure.

'A mouthful of bread, a cup of tea, and I'm away again!' he announced.

'Best not show him that letter yet!' Shane decided.

'Bridgie and I are off to buy a doll after tea!' said Mrs O'Clery. 'Maybe the boys can mind the shop!'

Her husband smiled and glanced happily at a thin, battered volume lying beside his plate. They knew he wasn't thinking of the shop.

Patrick stood in the doorway watching his mother and Bridgie as they went up the quay, the little girl walking as sedately as an old woman instead of jumping and dancing as she usually did.

'Wish I could have found Migeen for her!' he said. 'It's very strange.'

'You did your best,' Shane told him.

'I didn't find it!' grumbled Patrick.

He opened his schoolbag and started on his homework. Shane watched the long slender fingers grip the pen and write graceful flowing characters.

Shane had been the best scholar at Ballylicky National School but, compared with Patrick, he knew nothing, and Patrick was two years younger. If he wrote, his carefully formed letters were square and clumsy. Mrs O'Clery had said the author of *Gulliver's Travels* was the cleverest man the country had known. Yet look at his queer writing!

Shane watched Patrick's pen travelling quickly across the page. He had never seen such beautiful writing before.

'Your mother says you'll be an artist!' he murmured.

Patrick smiled over at him.

'I'm going to the School of Art when I leave North King Street,' he said. 'That's one reason I'm so glad you're here. Only for you I'd have to work in the shop when I'm too old for school!'

He bent over his books and Shane sat there, tingling with pride. The O'Clerys had, he was sure, taken him out of kindness. He might have been quite useless, yet already he was helping Patrick to be an artist. If only Uncle Tim could know. Aunt Maureen would be glad he had found friends and a roof over his head. But Uncle Tim would understand!

Where could he be? He must be having great adventures!

'If only I could be with him!' thought the boy.

Almost at once he realized that he was happy with the O'Clerys and would hate to leave them, even to be with Uncle Tim!

Patrick slapped his books together and stowed them in his bag.

'Do you mind if I go off for a bit?' he asked.

'Not at all!' replied Shane, delighted to be left in charge.

He sat there dreaming until a strange voice called:

'Say! Is there anyone looking after this shop?'

The boy ran out to find a tall man sitting on one of the tables gazing round him.

'You reckon on folks being mighty honest in these parts!' he said, in a soft, drawling voice. 'I could have carried off an armful of books!'

'I should have been here!' confessed Shane. 'What can I do for you?'

'There's a fine *Gulliver's Travels* in the window. How much is it?'

Shane sighed. But he felt thankful there was another copy and he was eager to sell all he could.

'I think Mr O'Clery is asking five guineas!' he said. 'Could you wait a while or could you come tomorrow? He's gone out and I'd sooner you bought the book from him. I haven't been here long and I don't know a deal about selling yet.'

'I'll wait!' the man told him.

'Would you care to look at the book while you're waiting?' asked Shane.

He was trying to be a good salesman, but he had never yet sold a book for more than a few shillings and he was nervous about selling one of the more expensive books in the shop.

The man nodded, slipped from the table, and settled himself in Mr O'Clery's chair. Shane lifted the book carefully from the window and placed it before him.

'It's a grand story!' said Shane. 'It's a bit hard to read but you'll like it!'

The customer leaned back.

'Even if I do buy it, son, I won't read it! I'm interested in the author, the great Dean Swift! He lived in these parts. I don't mind telling you, I'd sooner have two words written in that man's hand than all the famous books he wrote.'

Shane stared at the stranger. Leaning over, he turned the pages and pulled out the sheet of paper he had found, showing it to the man.

'*Jonath: Swift.*'

He looked up at the boy.

'Say, son! Is this his signature?'

Shane nodded.

'Why isn't it locked up?' cried the man. 'Why isn't it in a museum? I can't understand you folks in this country! You leave treasures lying about as if you didn't care! You let fine old houses that belong to history drop to ruin and now you fetch out a great man's signature as if it was an order for ink or pencils! A boy like you shouldn't be showing that around. It might be stolen! I don't want to be personal but in my country – I expect you've guessed I'm an American – we have a respect for antiquity! Your Mr – what's his name – O'Clery, must be a very careless man!'

Shane did not speak.

'Now, son, what would he want for this?' asked the American.

Shane shivered.

'He didn't say!'

The American half-closed his eyes and put his head on one side.

'I wonder would he consider twenty pounds?'

Shane gasped. Twenty pounds!

Surely even Uncle Tim had never had twenty pounds at one time! Most likely it would pay all the O'Clerys' debts! They'd be pleased. He thought of the way they would praise him.

'When will Mr O'Clery be back?' asked the man.

'I don't know!' replied Shane.

The stranger frowned.

'I can't wait any longer! I'm going to Killarney in the morning. Well, I think Jonathan Swift's signature is worth twenty pounds! How many dollars is that? Never mind! I'll be back in Dublin in a day or so and I'm staying at the Gresham in O'Connell Street. The name's David Forsythe. I'd like to put this in a safe place at once. If I leave the money with you, can you give me a receipt?'

He drummed on the table with his strong fingers.

'Of course I can!'

Shane knew where the book of receipts was kept – in a drawer of the old bureau in the corner. He tore one out. At the top was printed *Eugene O'Clery, The Four Masters' Bookshop, Bachelors' Walk, Dublin.* Underneath Shane wrote:

> Received from David Forsythe
> Staying at Gresham Hotel
> Twenty Pounds
> For Jonathan Swift's signature
> (Signed) SHANE MADDEN

He held it out. The American picked up an envelope and put the two pieces of paper carefully into it. He counted twenty pound notes into Shane's hand and scribbled his name on a sheet of paper.

'I'm more than pleased,' he said. 'I'll write Mr O'Clery when I get back home to Cincinnati, if I haven't time to see him.'

'Will you take the book?' asked Shane.

'No! No book! I've something much more important! I reckon I've made a bargain!'

He strode from the shop, walking proudly. Shane gazed after him with a bewildered face.

'Shall I put the money in the drawer for a surprise?' he asked himself.

His hand was on the drawer when Mrs O'Clery came into the shop with Bridgie trailing after her. They both looked cross and tired.

'Did you buy the doll?' asked Shane.

Mrs O'Clery took off her coat, hung it behind the door, and sank into her favourite chair.

'We did not!' she said. 'There wasn't a doll in the place that would satisfy Bridgie, not for the money I had.'

Shane felt the notes in his pocket. Should he bring them out now and tell about the American? Thoughtfully he decided to wait until Mr O'Clery returned.

Just then Patrick came in.

'Where's the new doll?' he asked.

'There isn't a doll in Dublin as good as Migeen!' declared Bridgie scornfully.

'We could put a notice in the window!' suggested Mrs O'Clery.

'I'll do one this very moment!' said Patrick.

They sat round the table watching him. He took a sheet of white cardboard and drew a picture of the puppet at the top and one of Migeen at the bottom. In between he printed:

LOST – *A Remarkable Puppet Dressed In Red With A Black Shawl. Mislaid On Bachelors' Walk. Reward Offered. Apply Within*

He replaced the big *Gulliver's Travels* in the window and stuck the notice on the glass in front of it. Bridgie began to smile.

'Do you remember when dadda lost his note-book and Patrick put up a notice and next day people were bringing note-books and note-books, but never the right one?' she asked.

'I do indeed!' sighed Mrs O'Clery. 'Let's hope we won't be buried under puppets and rag dolls!'

16. Shadows on the Quays

'Time ye were in yer bed, Bridgie!' said Mrs Flanagan. 'Go up now! Who knows, ye might dream of poor Migeen. Wouldn't that be grand?'

Silently Bridgie picked up the cat and climbed to the wide landing above the room. She went more slowly on the spiral staircase leading to the attic. As she pushed the door behind her, Mog stretched himself on the bed while Bridgie curled up on the window seat and looked out.

Her mother's voice came up to her – 'Say your prayers and jump into bed!'

'In a minute!' murmured Bridgie.

There was frost on the pane and she shivered. Her thick winter coat was lying beside her. She pulled it on and, squeezing into the corner, began to feel warm again.

Presently she heard the boys coming up, then her father and mother. Last of all, Mrs Flanagan's slow, weary steps went past her door.

'Good night, pet!' she heard. 'Sleep well!'

Bridgie breathed on the window and rubbed a patch of the glass clear. The quays were deserted, the stone parapets powdered with frost. The Liffey shone like a stream of silver and the shadows were so distinct they looked more real and solid than the houses, churches, bridges.

One shadow moved away from the others. It was small,

near the ground. It didn't look like a dog or cat. Bridgie was puzzled. What could it be?

'It looks like my Migeen! It can't be! Bu –'

The small shadow stopped in the roadway.

'Mog! Come down to the shop with me!' whispered Bridgie. 'I can see better from the window there.'

She opened the attic door as softly as she could and crept down the winding stair. From the landing, Bridgie looked over the wide balustrade into the big room. The lights were switched off but there was still a glow from the fire. She could see the chairs pushed back, schoolbags lying on the settle, and her mother's knitting on an open book.

Mog glided before her down to the warm room and stalked into the darkness of the shop.

'Don't like the dark!' murmured Bridgie. But she followed the cat.

She couldn't see from the windows. She had forgotten the shutters.

'We must go back to bed!' she said, yawning.

Mog rubbed his head against the door and miaowed.

'Want to go out?' asked Bridgie.

'Mee-ow!' replied Mog, waving his bushy tail.

'Want me to open the door? I'll soon do that!' she boasted.

The bolt at the bottom was easy enough. The other was too high.

Bridgie began to drag one of the chairs across the floor. It was so big and heavy, the noise it made startled her.

'Best go up to bed!' she decided.

Mog darted suddenly across the shop, through the big room, and into the kitchen. A pleasant smell of sausages and toast lingered there. The cat's tail twitched but the door into the yard was ajar and out he went. Bridgie followed, very slowly.

The high gate in the wall was only latched. In a moment they were through and the gate drawn gently behind them.

The silence and loneliness frightened Bridgie. She stared up the street, where the tall houses stood out like black-and-white drawings against the star-spangled sky. They seemed unreal without people at the windows, in the doorways, and on the street. A cold wind tossed Bridgie's hair and she hugged her coat closer.

Mog rubbed against her ankles, then trotted towards the river, looking back as he reached the wide doorway of the shop.

'We must go back!' said Bridgie. 'I never meant to come this far!'

Yet she went forward.

The tapping of her boots sounded so clear and distinct she expected windows to be thrown open and voices cry out:

'Is that Bridgie O'Clery abroad at night – and all alone?' 'You should be in your bed, Bridgie O'Clery! You should be in your bed!'

Mog paused at the corner of the shop and sat down.

As Bridgie reached him she made a grab, but the little cat was off across the roadway. He stood watching, his head on one side.

'It would be fun if Patrick was here,' thought Bridgie. 'What's happened to all the people? Why should everyone be in bed?'

The window opened above her and she heard Shane's voice – urgent, alarmed!

'That's not a shadow! That's Bridgie! I'll call her!'

'No!' came Patrick's clear voice. 'Don't rouse the others! We'll bring her back. Maybe she's walking in her sleep. She did once, when she was little! Hurry!'

'I won't go back without Mog!' thought Bridgie. 'And I do believe that's Migeen along there! Yet how can it be?'

Bridgie ran across the road but Mog was away on the bridge, and behind her she heard the opening and closing of the yard gate, then the boys' boots clattering on the pavement.

Bridgie stood still and they came up, one on each side.

'What possessed you, Bridgie?' asked her brother. 'Come back at once!'

'Look!' said Bridgie.

Mog was stepping daintily across the bridge and uttering delighted little mee-ows of excitement.

'He's often out at night, as you well know!' declared Patrick, longing to follow, yet determined to be sensible.

Shane looked farther and pointed.

'What's that?' he asked in a startled whisper.

They stared at the tiny figure in front of Mog, black shawl fluttering as it skipped and whirled, like a dry leaf in the wind.

'It's my Migeen!' said Bridgie. 'At first I couldn't be sure!'

'It can't be!' exclaimed Patrick.

As Bridgie looked she felt sure. No one understood why she had such an affection for a battered rag doll. But Bridgie knew Migeen was far more important than the grand dolls with blue eyes and golden hair in the shops of Henry Street and O'Connell Street. Sometimes she had been sure Migeen was smiling at her and trying to talk. So now when Bridgie saw the little puppet skipping and jumping over the bridge she wasn't as surprised as Patrick.

Migeen looked far grander than in the days before she became a puppet. Her red dress made a splash of colour like an
autumn leaf as she danced along in the moonlight.

'Of course it's my Migeen!' said Bridgie. 'I always knew
she was a clever doll. She's bound to be a clever puppet.'

They moved slowly across the bridge. Bridgie danced between the boys, clinging to their hands. No longer frightened,
she thought how lovely night could be, better even than day!

'I don't understand!' murmured Shane.

'We should go back!' said Patrick.

But they kept on. The quays were deserted. Out of sight
they heard the steady tread of a guard. A faint hiss and splash
rose from the river, where a cluster of swans drifted with the
tide. The lines of lights along the quays and the bridges were
faint in the moonlight and the scent of burnt turf mingled with
the muddy, salty smell of the Liffey.

'Puppets can't walk by themselves!' protested Shane.

He thought longingly of the snug bed on the far side of the
river. It seemed a long way off.

They mounted the rise of Winetavern Street where the old,
crumbling shops and houses were closed and dark. Above
them, in the shadow of Christ Church Cathedral, beneath the
lovely grey arch which spans the roadway, stood a man gazing
down at the moonlit Liffey.

The tiny figure of the moving puppet stopped in the gutter
at his feet. Mog pounced and crouched beside it. Bridgie drew
back, gripping Patrick's warm hand tightly.

Shane was puzzled. The man's face seemed familiar. Yet
where could he have seen such queer clothes?

He was accustomed to seeing men in black gowns and white
wigs hurrying across the courtyard of the Four Courts on
Ormond Quay. But this stranger was not one of them!

He wore a wig, as they did. But not one among them had a
coat with widely cuffed sleeves, reaching to the knees and
hanging open to show an embroidered vest. Who in Dublin

wore knee-breeches, with long stockings and thick, low-heeled, buckled shoes?

'Yet I've seen him before!' thought Shane.

Suddenly he remembered a picture hanging at the back of

the shop – the picture of a man very like this one. On a slip of cardboard stuck into the frame was printed, in Patrick's beautiful writing

Jonathan Swift – Dean of St Patrick's

Mr O'Clery had shown this to Shane his second day at the Four Masters' Bookshop.

'There is Dublin's greatest writer,' he told the boy.

Shane clutched Bridgie's hand. He longed to turn and run down the hill, back over the bridge into the safety of the shop and yet he knew he would never forget this moment as long as he lived.

The strange, familiar face, sad and strong; the queer clothes! Was he dreaming or was the great Dean Swift really looking over the city he had served so well?

'Ye should be in your beds!' said the stranger, in a deep voice. 'Do children still roam the streets of Dublin at night, homeless and uncared for? Yet ye haven't the look of vagrants. Why are ye abroad so late at night?'

'Twas my fault!' explained Bridgie. 'My doll, Migeen, that's her, has been turned into a puppet. Mog, that's the cat, followed her! I followed Mog and the boys followed me!'

'A bold lass!' said the man, smiling. 'Weren't ye afraid?'

'Indeed I was!' replied Bridgie. 'It was the puppet frightened me! When Migeen was a doll, she never went walking by herself!'

'Yet ye're not frightened now?'

'Why would I be? Haven't I Patrick and Shane here to take care of me, and you wouldn't let anything hurt us, would you?'

'I would not!' cried the man. 'I would protect ye as I tried to protect all the children of Dublin! Ye, who have no fear of the man who once lived here, who was lonely and unhappy!'

'We have a picture of you in our shop!' Patrick told him eagerly. 'My father says you were one of the great men of Dublin!'

'So ye know me?' asked the man.

'You are Jonathan Swift, Dean of St Patrick's!' said Shane slowly.

To himself he was thinking: 'It can't be! It can't be! I'm dreaming!'

'And I – bitter and disappointed – thought I was forgotten! But even the children remember me!' said Dean Swift.

'Of course we do!' cried Bridgie. 'Haven't we your book in our window – the one about the giants and the little people and the talking horses? Sure we all know that!'

The man lifted his head and glanced backward at Christ Church.

'So the Dean of St Patrick's still lives! I am remembered! Yet what does it matter? I did my work!'

'It matters to us!' said Patrick proudly.

The Dean towered above them, dark and grand in the moonlight.

'You really are Jonathan Swift!' whispered Shane in wonder.

The three drew closer together.

The great man smiled down at them.

'So I, the Dean of St Patrick's, still have power! Here are three who will never forget me! But this – is it real? Is it alive? Can it be a Lilliputian?'

He stooped and caught up the puppet. It bowed and tossed its head. As they laughed, in the distance a voice sang:

> 'One moonlight night, by the Liffey river,
> I walked alone, not a soul with me.
> I saw the great ones in all their glory;
> Twas those who died to make Ireland free.'

Dean Swift handed Migeen to Bridgie.

'Take good care of your treasure!' he told her. 'Now I must be on my way to St Patrick's! Ye three have given me hope! There may be others who remember!'

He turned his back on them. His straight, proud figure strode into the shadows of the archway. A cloud darkened the moon and when it passed, Shane, Patrick, and Bridgie stood there, silent and wondering, for the road lay empty before them.

'We should be home!' said Patrick, shivering.

Mog sprang down Winetavern Street. Bridgie stumbled after, carrying the puppet, now limp and lifeless. Shane and Patrick marched last, their footsteps echoing and re-echoing.

Patrick fumbled with the latch of the yard door and pushed in the bolts.

'You won't do this again, will you?' he asked his sister.

She blinked but didn't answer.

They crept into the big room. Bridgie went up first. Dropping her clothes on the floor, she tumbled into bed, Migeen clutched in her hands and Mog stretched beside her.

The boys took off their boots at the foot of the stairs.

'Were you afraid?' whispered Patrick.

'Maybe I was!' admitted Shane. 'I'm terribly cold and sleepy.'

17. Next Morning Courage

When Shane woke in the morning he had forgotten the happenings of the night before. He was opening the door to go downstairs when he noticed Patrick leaning from the window and gazing across the river.

'Anything wrong?' he asked, looking over the other boy's shoulder.

'I was thinking of Dean Swift!' murmured Patrick.

'That's queer!' said Shane. 'I dreamt of him!'

'Are you sure it was a dream?' asked Patrick.

Shane looked thoughtfully at his companion.

'I dreamt Bridgie ran out with Mog, chasing her lost puppet. We followed her up Winetavern Street and, at the top under the arch, we met the man who wrote *Gulliver's Travels*.'

Patrick smiled.

'I went with you and we did meet Dean Swift! It wasn't a dream. It was real!'

'How could it be?' asked Shane.

'Hurry, lads!' called Mr O'Clery. 'Breakfast's on the table!'

They went down. Bridgie was there blinking with sleepiness. Mog lay on one side of her, the puppet sprawled limply on the other.

Mrs O'Clery poured out tea, as the Widow Flanagan came in with a dish of boiled eggs.

'Boiled eggs!' exclaimed Mr O'Clery in disgust. 'Like as not they'll be raw and watery!'

'Be thankful tis not dry bread ye're eating, and glad to have it!' cried the widow. 'They're all I could get and ye owing money up and down the place. Now why don't ye stop buying books and get down to selling them ye have! Look at them! We've hardly room to turn! I've a mind to give up cooking and cleaning and get behind the counter meself! Me and young Shane would make a fist of the shop, so we would!'

She put down the dish of eggs and started back.

''Pon me soul! Ye've found the puppet! Where, Bridgie, where?'

'On the quay!' replied Bridgie.

'When? When, child? Ah, tell me when ye're awake!'

'A few rashers would make a deal of difference!' declared the bookseller. 'Or why not fry the eggs? That wouldn't ruin us, surely?'

Shane sat up very straight. He put his hand in his pocket and pulled out the roll of notes.

'These belong to you, Mr O'Clery!' he said, pushing them across the table.

The bookseller stopped tapping his egg to stare at the crumpled notes. He poked them with his finger.

'You couldn't have taken that amount for books!' he said. 'How much is there?'

'Twenty pounds!' answered Shane.

'Twenty pounds!' cried Mr O'Clery, his eyes opening wide.

Mrs Flanagan, slapping a dish of hot buttered toast on the table, leaned over.

'Isn't it grand to see a bit of money around the place again!' she sighed. 'I knew that lad would bring us luck! Twenty pounds! Now ye'll be able to pay off a few debts! Leave the shop to Shane Madden and ye'll be driving a car down the quays before any of us are much older!'

'Which books did you sell?' asked Mr O'Clery anxiously. 'I hope you didn't touch the first editions?'

He looked up at his shelf of treasures. They were still packed tight. He smiled with relief.

'Out with it, lad! Speak up! I won't eat you! What books did you sell?'

'It wasn't books!' said Shane. 'It was a signature!'

'Whose signature? We haven't a signature worth twenty pounds in the shop!' said Mr O'Clery scornfully. 'We haven't have we, Eilis?'

Mrs O'Clery shook her head thoughtfully.

'Not to my knowledge!' she replied.

'Tell us, Shane!' urged Patrick. 'Whose was it?'

Still Shane hesitated. Bridgie waved her spoon with the egg dripping from it and shrieked joyfully.

'I know! I know! Jonathan Swift! Jonathan Swift! The man who wrote *Gulliver's Travels*. We met him last night and I expect he knows all about it. He knows everything!'

'Stop screaming, Bridgie!' ordered Mrs O'Clery. 'And put down your spoon! Behave like a civilized human being or I'll put you and your precious Mog out in the yard, and the puppet too!'

'Bridgie's right!' said Shane. 'I sold Dean Swift's signature for twenty pounds!'

Mr O'Clery bit off a huge mouthful of toast.

'My dear boy!' he said. 'You couldn't have sold a signature of Dean Swift's. We never had one! If we had, it would have been framed and hung up there beside his picture. What did you sell?'

'Whatever twas, ye'd never have the sense to sell it yerself!' grumbled Mrs Flanagan. 'Can I have some of that money, ma'am, to put us out of danger?'

'Yes! Yes!' cried Mrs O'Clery. 'Here, take five pounds! Surely that's enough!'

'Something to go on with!' muttered the widow. 'I'll make a list and get young Patrick to add it up for me!'

She went smiling into the kitchen.

'I sold Jonathan Swift's signature!' persisted Shane. 'I found it in *Gulliver's Travels* and I meant to show it you. It's on a kind of a letter.'

Mr O'Clery bolted the last of his egg.

'We had no letter of Swift's! I wish we had! I'd sooner have it than anything else, almost!'

Patrick leaned across the table.

'Was it about an apprentice?' he asked eagerly.

Shane nodded.

'That's it!'

'But it's only a copy – a kind of copy!' explained the younger boy. 'Don't you remember, dadda? You had a book about Swift and in it was a copy of a letter he wrote recommending a boy as an apprentice. You gave me a piece of old paper and I made a copy. I meant to show it you but I lost it!'

'It dropped out of *Gulliver's Travels*!' said Shane. 'I sold it and, if it's only a copy, I suppose I cheated the man!'

'You didn't know!' exclaimed Mrs O'Clery. 'How could you? But the man should have known!'

Patrick looked around him with pride.

'When I make a copy, there isn't one could tell it from the original just by looking at it!' he said.

'You mean that you, Patrick, copied Dean Swift's signature and you, Shane, sold it as a genuine autograph?' cried Mr O'Clery in amazement.

'I copied it!' replied Patrick.

'I sold it!' murmured Shane.

'Make no more copies, Patrick!' said his father gravely. 'You see what's happened. You've turned Shane into a cheat! We must give the money back! Mrs Flanagan! We can't use that money!'

Bridgie thumped the table with her spoon.

'You leave Shane alone!' she cried indignantly. 'He didn't cheat! He only wanted us to have some money so I could have a doll and Mrs Flanagan wouldn't be bothered! And he doesn't cheat!'

'If I have any more of this boldness, Bridgie, I'll slap you!' said her mother.

Mrs Flanagan came in flushed and upset.

'Now, Mr O'Clery! Don't ask me to give this money back! We need it! If ye don't take a grip on yerselves, we'll all be starving. And stop giving out to young Shane. He's as good a boy as Patrick!'

She bent over Bridgie.

'Never dream yer mammy would lay a hand on ye, pet! She was only letting on, God help her!'

'I could scream and make a show of her!' suggested Bridgie cheerfully.

'That ye could ye young heartscald! But ye wouldn't! Ye have a bit of pride!'

'What are we to do with this money?' asked Mr O'Clery.

'Sure, it won't bite ye!' snapped Mrs Flanagan. 'I might have known twas too good to be true! Though why we shouldn't have a scrap of money, dear knows! And all the other shops coining, just coining!'

'What's this man's name and where does he live?' asked Mrs O'Clery.

Shane tried to remember.

'Did you give him a receipt for his money?' the bookseller wanted to know. 'Ah now, Shane, I told you always to give one for over ten shillings. Surely you did that?'

'He was an American!' said Shane slowly, trying to remember. 'He's staying at an hotel in O'Connell Street, and his name is – is –'

'That will be the Gresham!' decided Mrs O'Clery. 'All the Americans stay there! If only you knew his name!'

Patrick had left his breakfast to search among the papers on his father's desk. Shane watched how he stacked answered letters at one side, unanswered at the other, bills in front.

'Here we are!' he cried, holding up a sheet of paper with a printed heading – *Eugene O'Clery, The Four Masters' Book-shop, Bachelors' Walk, Dublin.*

His father snatched it from him.

'Daniel Forsythe!' he read out loud. 'Cincinnati, Ohio, U.S.A.'

'Shane! You go to the hotel and find him!' said Mrs O'Clery. 'Give him the money back and explain. Tell him you didn't understand!'

'I should have known!' said Shane. 'I'm terribly ashamed!'

'My dear boy! How could you understand?' spluttered Mr O'Clery, eating toast rapidly so that he would be able to speak more distinctly. 'You do now and you're sorry! You can make amends and there'll be no harm done! I'm afraid it's all my fault. If I were a better shopkeeper, if I gave my mind to selling books, this wouldn't have happened. You wanted to get money for us and you didn't know about Patrick's non-sense.'

Shane sat up suddenly.

'Mr O'Clery, I remember now! The American was going to Killarney but he was coming back to Dublin!'

The bookseller sighed.

'I'll go with you and explain! I can't leave that to you!'

Shane settled himself in his chair and ate the egg which Mrs Flanagan had put out for him. It was cold but he thought it the best egg he had ever tasted. With Mr O'Clery to do the explaining he had nothing to worry about and he was de-lighted at the chance of seeing the inside of the Gresham.

'It's a palace, that's what it is!' he thought.

Then he noticed Mr O'Clery's serious face.

'He hates going there and it's not fair he should have to!' decided Shane.

He leaned across the table.

'Don't you bother to come, Mr O'Clery! I'll go by myself! I can tell everything and ask Mr Forsythe to come here to see you. If he's not there, I can leave a message.'

'Are you sure you don't mind?' asked the bookseller anxiously.

'Not a bit!' declared Shane.

They stood in the doorway as he set off down the quays. While they were watching he walked quickly. When he looked back and discovered they had gone inside his steps became slower and slower. By the time he reached O'Connell Bridge he felt he had tramped miles.

'Wish Mr O'Clery had come!' said Shane to himself. 'Maybe the American won't be there! Wasn't it today he was going to Killarney? Then I can go back, no harm done, and I can leave a message.'

Shane crossed at the Nelson Pillar with the crowd. He studied them enviously. They weren't worried about money, or copied names, or anything serious. Yet, when he looked again, not all of them seemed happy. Some were tired already. There was one man on crutches, though he was whistling cheerfully. One woman, pushing a pram, was coaxing a fat little boy to keep with her. Shane took his hand and brought him across the road. The more he noticed, the more he saw people who were fighting their troubles. Even the women selling flowers and fruit on the stalls at the foot of the

Pillar were being beaten by the wind and their red hands were so cold they could scarcely count out the change.

Now he was at the entrance to the Gresham. In spite of the bitter wind, people were sitting in the arm-chairs outside, under the portico. The American wasn't there. Shane went up the steps between the pillars and followed a porter carrying luggage through swinging glass doors.

Inside, a messenger about his own size, in a blue uniform and wearing white gloves, stood before him.

'Want anyone?' asked the boy, gazing haughtily over Shane's head.

'Mr Daniel Forsythe. I've a message for him.'

'Wait here!' ordered the messenger, and pushed through another pair of swing doors.

Shane stood gazing into the lounge where cushioned seats and little tables were scattered over the crimson carpet. He saw waiters dressed in black and white, waitresses who seemed to him even more elegant than the ladies in furs. He heard a buzz of talk and in the distance a high-pitched voice crying out: 'Mr Daniel Forsythe! Mr Dan-iel For-sythe, please!'

The messenger returned.

'Not there!' he said. 'But he was here and he's kept his room. You can write a message!'

So Shane stood at a counter where bags and trunks were being passed across and wrote a note asking Mr Daniel Forsythe to call at The Four Masters' Bookshop. He gave one last admiring glance at the glittering chandeliers, the wide staircases, the arches leading on and on, went through the swing doors, down the steps, back into crowded O'Connell Street.

He was disappointed and relieved, tired and excited. He ran all the way back to the quays.

Mr O'Clery had locked up the money in his desk and was peacefully reading in the shop. Patrick and Bridgie were at school. Mog was stretched on the magazines at the door. Mrs

Flanagan was singing in the kitchen and Mrs O'Clery was winding wool in the big room.

'The American wasn't there, ma'am!' said Shane. 'I left a message. He's coming back!'

'There's a good lad!' said Mrs O'Clery, without looking up.

She had forgotten the twenty pounds!

18. Hallowe'en

When there were no customers Shane arranged the books on the shelves so that he found room for those on the floor and on the tables.

This made the shop look so much larger that he set to work on those in the big room. They were stacked everywhere – on the floor, on the window-seats. Even the settle in the corner was crowded above and below.

'There should be shelves!' grumbled Shane. 'If we had shelves all along that side right up to the ceiling we'd have heaps of room!'

'Not for long!' declared Patrick, looking up from lettering a map of the Aran Islands he was drawing for his homework. 'There'll be more books and more books. You'll see!'

'If Uncle Tim was here he'd make shelves!' declared Shane. 'You should see the ones he fixed for Aunt Maureen. They were better than any in Cork! Stained and polished, and all from boxes!'

He sat gazing into the fire, wishing his uncle was beside him.

'The things we could do together!' he thought.

Mrs Flanagan saw the veil of sadness steal over his face.

'The poor lad's lonesome! Thinking of that rapscallion of an uncle, no doubt!' she told herself.

She shifted her chair.

'Why don't ye make the shelves yerself?' she asked. 'I'd

lend a hand and so would young Patrick here, wouldn't ye, avic? We can move the settee over be the winda! Then, there'll be lashings of space!'

Patrick looked up from his map.

'I'll make the stain, and I'll do the staining!' he offered.

'I'll do the polishing!' said Bridgie mournfully.

She was working on a page of sums, with Mog half on the chair, half on her lap. The puppet was propped behind her.

'Ye'll do no such thing!' cried Mrs Flanagan. 'I'll not give ye a chance to put as much polish on yer face as on the shelves! Don't we all know ye hate real honest work the way the divil hates Holy water!'

'Where will I get the wood?' asked Shane.

'Isn't there dozens of boxes, not to mind the good, strong packing cases, out back there in the yard? I've me poor husband's tools eating their heads off up in me room! Let ye pull out the nails and the work's half done, no sawing, and that's the hardest.'

'I'll start in the morning!' said Shane.

Patrick went to school reluctantly.

'Don't do too much!' he warned Shane. 'Leave some for me!'

Mr O'Clery was going to see a customer about some first editions.

'I'll hate to part with them!' he lamented. 'Yet I am a bookseller! It's my job! Shane! While you're making shelves, don't forget the shop!'

'I'll help the lad keep an eye on it!' promised Mrs Flanagan. 'And Mr O'Clery! Don't be late for the bit of dinner! There's half a pig's cheek and a slab of white cabbage. Ye'll like that – there's no bones in it! Tell the missus if ye meet her on the quay. She's out doing the shopping, God help her! Now she'll know what I go through!'

Before Shane had drawn out a dozen nails, he wished he had not been so sure he could make shelves. It had seemed easy when Uncle Tim did the work. He could draw out nails so that they were as straight as when they came from the shop. The little heap Shane had gathered were all bent and twisted.

'God be good to us!' cried Mrs Flanagan when she looked out to see how the work was progressing. 'Sure ye haven't the knack wid them fellas! Let me take a hand! I've watched me poor man at the job many a time. Look now! Steady the box wid yer foot. Give a lift to the nail wid them pincers. Now to the right. Now to the left and pull!'

She held the nail up proudly. It wasn't quite straight. But it was perfect compared with Shane's attempts.

He tried to do the same – pulling and easing, gently and steadily. Every few moments she came from the kitchen to help and Shane was grateful.

'Sure, child, carpentry's a skilled job and ye can't go at it like splitting a log of wood. Ye must work slow and learn each bit. Ye're doing grand wid the nails. Now give a lift at your end while I lift at mine. There's the first shelf – a bit short but ye can have two or mebbe three, side by side!'

'Putting them up will be the hard part!' said Shane doubtfully.

'We'll face that when we come to it! We might get the master to give us a helping hand. Though, dear knows, tis that man's head I'd trust, not his hands!'

Patrick came rushing in, Bridgie panting to keep up with him.

'How much have you done?' demanded Patrick.

He looked at the settle.

'Shall I help you move it?' he asked eagerly.

Shane made a face.

'It's not so easy as I thought! I've only one shelf ready to put up and it's too short!'

'Why not use orange boxes?' asked Mrs O'Clery, who had returned without going into a single shop. 'Pile them on one another. They'll be safe and strong! If you smooth and stain them, they'll look as good as any shelves you could make when the books are on them.'

'Bless and save us, ma'am!' cried Mrs Flanagan indignantly. 'That's no way to treat books! Tis only tinkers would do that!'

Shane flushed.

'There'll be no need to use orange boxes!' he said proudly. 'I'll make proper shelves.'

Mr O'Clery came in while they were all helping Mrs Flanagan to lay the table. He looked tired and dejected.

'Sit down!' said his wife. 'You need a good meal and it's ready. Wouldn't the man agree to take the books?'

'He did and he agreed to the price we decided. He's paid me in advance!'

Mrs O'Clery smiled.

'That's good! Now Shane needn't feel the least regret over the American's money. But what's troubling you?'

The bookseller flung his hat and coat on the settle.

'I hate parting with books, real books!' he grumbled. 'If they were new I wouldn't mind. One new book is like all its comrades, but an old book has a history apart from what's in it.'

'New books are best!' crooned Bridgie. 'New books are best!'

Her father looked at her severely.

'Let's hope when you're older you'll have more sense!' he said.

'I can't help being glad we have some money!' confessed Mrs O'Clery. 'This morning I was ashamed to go into a single shop!'

Mrs Flanagan put a big plate before Mr O'Clery. It was piled with thin pink slices of pig's cheek. The chopped white cabbage sent up a fragrant steam. The potatoes were balls of flour. He pulled in his chair and smiled.

'Mind ye, there's something in what the child says!' declared Mrs Flanagan. 'She has a head on her, has young

Bridgie! If ye'd fill the winda wid books that look bright and sticky ye'd sell them! Then ye could keep the old ones back here and spend yer remaining days wid them!'

'New books are best!' whispered Bridgie to Mog, who purred loudly.

Maybe he agreed; maybe he was just encouraging her to hurry with her dinner and hand him down the plate.

'If I weren't a good-tempered man,' said Mr O'Clery, lifting a delicious forkful to his mouth, 'I'd take Bridgie out and lose her!'

'Not without Mog and Migeen!' declared Bridgie.

She let a strip of pig's cheek dangle into the little cat's open mouth.

'Just a tiny bit, so you'll know how it tastes!' she whispered, and looked up to meet her father's frown.

'You wouldn't like it if you had to watch us all eating and eating, and you with nothing in your mouth!' she protested, while Mog squeezed closer.

'There's a difference!' declared the bookseller, trying not to laugh.

'It would be wonderful to sell new clean books!' said Patrick. 'As well as the others!' he added, with an anxious look at his father.

Mrs Flanagan took away the empty plates.

'Ye have a grand shop going to waste!' she said, over her shoulder. 'Them ones that buys the old books don't care a thraneen what's inside. Tis the binding, and the printing, and the mistakes, and the old age of them they're admiring, and that's an insult to the one that wrote the story. Ah, eat the good treacle pudding while it's hot and don't be annoying me!'

Mr O'Clery sighed.

'I wonder!' he said.

Bridgie was sorry for her father. If he liked old books best, why shouldn't he have what he wanted?

'*Gulliver's Travels* is as good old as new!' she told him. 'It's queer anyway!'

Mr O'Clery leaned over and rumpled her hair.

'You're queer yourself!' he told her, laughing.

While they were having a cup of tea after dinner, rain came lashing down along the quays. The last leaves swirled from the trees and were blown along in gleaming companies. One golden leaf danced in through the open door, spun round and out again.

'Patrick allanna! Will ye shut that shop door!' asked Mrs Flanagan. 'There'll be no customers in this storm!'

Patrick stared out.

'Need we go to school this afternoon? We'll be drowned and Bridgie has a sore throat. You have haven't you, Bridgie?'

Bridgie nodded and coughed obligingly.

'Put on your waterproofs and your Wellingtons!' ordered their mother. 'You're not made of sugar! Go quickly! The rain is easing off for a while!'

Mrs O'Clery believed in schooling. She had never been to school but had been taught at home. Mr O'Clery had been in boarding-schools all his young life. He thought day schools wonderful!

'Off you go!' he said, filling his pipe carefully. 'Be thankful to the people who spend their time trying to put a little knowledge into your heads!'

'Mog! You take care of Migeen!' Bridgie told the cat. 'Mebbe the night will be fine and we can go out again. Don't forget! It's Hallowe'en!'

'Did you hear that?' Mr O'Clery asked his wife.

She smiled but did not answer. She was mending a big book with torn, crimson leather binding. Her long thin fingers worked quickly and, when she had finished, there wasn't a sign of mending.

'There's something very comforting about a job well done!' she told Shane.

He looked over his shoulder.

'Do you mind if I use the saw, ma'am? Would the noise disturb you?'

'Not at all! I'll only be dusting books!'

The saw didn't make much noise. The hammering was worse. Mrs O'Clery went into the shop and stood looking out at the rain while her husband wrote letters and puffed smoke until his corner was hazy and comfortable.

'I'll have to give up keeping books for my own pleasure!' he said. 'I'm selfish to keep those first editions up there in the 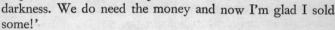 darkness. We do need the money and now I'm glad I sold some!'

That night Mr and Mrs O'Clery were going off to the Abbey Theatre to see a play about 'the Troubles' and they wouldn't be back until late.

'You can close early!' the bookseller told Shane. 'Who'll come buying books on Hallowe'en!'

As Shane brought in the cheaper books and magazines from outside, where he had put a piece of oil-cloth over them, he could hear Bridgie running backwards and forwards from her attic to Mrs Flanagan's.

The widow had disappeared. But her deep laugh came floating down the stairs. With a hammer in one hand and some rusty nails in the other, the boy sat back on his heels, listening. He was despairing of fixing the shelves so that they would hold books, yet he was ashamed to confess defeat.

'What are you up to?' he asked, as an apparition, draped in an old sheet, looked down at him from the landing.

'I'm a banshee!' announced Bridgie. 'Listen!'

She gave a howl which made Shane drop the hammer, while Patrick's sheets of drawing paper were scattered over the floor.

Bridgie came down the stairs, stepping carefully. After her came Mrs Flanagan, three grinning masks dangling from her fingers.

'If ye lads are going, ye should be ready!' she said. 'Ye know the young ones from North King Street will be calling

for ye, Patrick. Bridgie says ye promised. I've brought two of the missus's summer frocks. Bridgie's are too small!'

'I want to finish my map!' protested Patrick reluctantly.

'I'm too big!' muttered Shane.

'Ye'll have great sport on Hallowe'en down in the country!' said the widow. 'But the poor Dublin chisellers do the best they can!'

Shane was ashamed to explain that Uncle Joe would never let his family share in the Hallowe'en fun. Mrs Flanagan pulled a flowered silk frock over the boy's head and bunched it round the middle. Then he helped Patrick while Mrs Flanagan sat with her elbows on the table, laughing at them.

'If I were a few generations younger I'd be with ye!' she told them. 'Sure, I pity that young Imelda who can't go gallivanting on Hallowe'en, or out with the Wren Boys on St Stephen's Day. She's too grand for that – her father being a solicitor that carries an umbrella every day of his life, wet or fine, God help him! Be thankful, the three of ye, that Mr O'Clery is only a poor bookseller!'

'Come with us! Come with us!' cried Bridgie. 'Stoop down, Mrs Flanagan, and, in the dark, no one will know you're a grown-up woman! You can find another sheet and I'll let you have my mask. I'll just make faces! Only you'll have to howl like a banshee!'

'Ye dote!' cried the widow. 'Ye have me sorely tempted! But I have to hand out the apples and nuts! Ye and yer friends aren't the only ones who'll be demanding gifts tonight! Besides, I have to keep the fire in and the kettle on the boil. The master and herself will be famished when they get back from the play.'

'I've never been to a play!' said Shane regretfully.

Bridgie put her hand in his.

'Never mind! When Christmas comes, we'll all go to the pantomime at the Gaiety and you'll see Jimmy O'Dea! He'll be better than any play ever seen!'

There came a hammering at the shop door.

'Here are the young vagabones!' cried Mrs Flanagan. 'Throw open the door, Shane!'

There was a scuffling and chattering at the shop door and, as Shane stared out, a group of strangely dressed creatures appeared. Girls were dressed as boys, boys as girls, with bundled ill-fitting garments, some with blackened faces, some with masks. Girls were in their fathers' coats which reached to their heels, boys had borrowed their grandmothers' capes and bonnets. They all carried bags, baskets, or boxes.

Forming a semicircle on the pavement, they sang as loudly as they could:

'Mrs O'Clery! Mrs O'Clery! Please fill up our bags.
Give us apples and nuts for our Hallowe'en feast.
Give us all you can spare and we'll bring you good luck,
Or just a good wish and we won't mind the least!
Hip! Hip! Hip! Hooray!'

Mrs Flanagan came forward with the chipped enamel washing-up bowl filled with hazel nuts, almonds, chestnuts, walnuts, and small rosy apples.

'Mrs O'Clery left these for ye!' she explained. 'So take good care of the young one I'm letting go wid ye. In yer turn now! No pushing or shoving!'

The children stood patiently while she shared out the fruit. Then calling: 'Thank you, ma'am! Happy Hallowe'en, Mrs Flanagan! Tell Mrs O'Clery we were asking for her! Come along, Bridgie! Step out, Patsy, and bring the stranger boy!'

With a banshee wail Bridgie danced along, Shane and Patrick following. At first they were a little ashamed, then, delighting in the freedom of their disguise, they sang and shouted with the others.

'Don't be too late!' they heard Mrs Flanagan warning them. Now they were out on the road, invading shops, knocking at house doors, singing their chant, cheering when they were welcomed, booing when an occasional door was slammed on them.

Up O'Connell Street they charged, down Parnell Street, along into Stoney Batter.

'Where are we making for?' asked Shane.

'To Mrs MacNally's!' Patrick told him. 'She'll have a kettle of tea and the biggest barm brack in Dublin for us!'

Shane almost turned back. He hadn't been near Mrs MacNally to ask for news of Uncle Tim and was shy of meeting her.

But there she was, standing in the open door, ready to welcome them.

Bridgie wailed her loudest and when the crowd sang:

'*Mrs MacNally! Mrs MacNally!*
    Fill our boxes and bags!'

Shane sang with them.

'Come in, girls and boys!' shouted Mrs MacNally. 'I'd have an empty house this night if it wasn't for ye! Come in and take off them hidgeous faces!'

The children pulled off the masks for one another, and the smallest squeezed through to the front.

'Ah, Bridgie O'Clery! Is it yerself, love? Aren't ye the great young one!' cried Mrs MacNally. 'And there's the clever brother that's going to be a terrible credit to the country one day! Now who's this strange lad? I don't know ye but I've seen ye before! Ye're no Dubliner! Speak up!'

'I'm Shane Madden!' said the boy. 'Tim Madden is me uncle! I came here looking for him when I first came up from Ballylicky!'

Mrs MacNally nodded.

'I remember now! So poor Tim Madden's yer uncle. The best drover of them all and the wildest! I have a grah for Tim Madden. He'll turn up in his own time! Now, ye over yonder, with a face like a ripe chemato! Come forward and give out yer name! I don't know ye!'

'He's Rusty Martin from Crumlin!' shouted a dozen voices. 'He's staying with his grannie over in High Street!'

'Then he has no right here!' declared Mrs MacNally. 'This is the North side and we want no Southerners!'

'Let him stay!' pleaded Bridgie. 'He's all alone and, if you do, I'll let my Migeen dance for you!'

She held up the puppet and it danced on her fingers.

'That's a quare-looking dolly ye have! Ah, sure, what's one stranger more or less!' decided Mrs MacNally. 'Rusty can stay!'

They sat on the floor around the fire. They ate the nuts and apples they had collected, sang, whistled, danced. Then they had mugs of hot tea and slices of barm brack.

By this time Mrs MacNally had fallen asleep. She sat in a huge arm-chair by the fire, her arms folded, her head hanging down.

'How much money is there?' asked Patrick.

Rusty Martin had charge of the money in a wooden box. He counted it out.

'Only pennies and ha'pennies!' he said disgustedly. 'Over in Crumlin, I bet they'd give us threepennies, mebbe six-pennies!'

'How much?' persisted Patrick.

'Forty pennies! Forty ha'pennies!'

'That's sixty pence – five shillings! How many of us are there?'

They counted heads.

'Twenty!' said Patrick. 'That's threepence each. Put it up on the mantelpiece! We had a feast and I wish we could leave more!'

To Shane's surprise no one objected. Rusty arranged the coppers on the mantelpiece. Patrick opened the door and they all filed into the street.

'Let out a banshee wail!' suggested Rusty. 'Just to cheer us up! You do it grand!'

Bridgie yawned, but wailed as loudly as she could.

'Sh!' exclaimed Patrick. 'Haven't you any manners? Do you want to rouse Mrs Mac-Nally after all she's done for us?'

They stood at the corner of North King Street, shivering and sleepy.

'Isn't it lucky there's no school waiting for us tomorrow!' said Patrick, glancing at the big grey building. 'Safe home all! You going our way, Rusty?'

They started off, walking in the centre of the road. Bridgie was stumbling along, half-asleep, until Shane offered her a piggy back. Her sheet trailed behind them and Rusty came last of all.

'Does your grannie know where you are?' asked Patrick.

Rusty shook his head.

'I daresn't tell her! She'd be mad at me coming over this side. Only me mammy and me da used to live up be the Daisy Market till we got the new house in Crumlin. It's terrible grand but lonesome!'

They reached the bookshop. The door was ajar.

'Don't go in till I'm over the bridge!' pleaded Rusty. 'I'm afeard of water when the moon shines on it. I'll be seeing you!'

'Safe home!' called Patrick when the boy was half-way across.

He turned and waved. Then ran out of sight.

'A nice time to come back!' said an indignant voice behind them.

There stood Mr O'Clery in his old grey dressing-gown puffing his pipe.

'I needn't ask where you've been!' he said. 'I suppose Mrs Flanagan put you up to it!'

He shook his head as he gazed at the bedraggled dresses they had forgotten, and lifted Bridgie from Shane's shoulder.

'Young gadabouts!' he murmured. 'Up to bed, all of you! Can you get yourself into bed, Bridgie?'

Without answering, she scrambled upstairs, clutching Migeen and dropping her sheet on the floor. They heard her door slam.

'Ah well!' said Mr O'Clery. 'We're only young once!'

19. The Burning of the Books

The boys went slowly up to bed, pulled off the crumpled frocks and poked them in a bundle behind the door, while Mr O'Clery dropped back into his chair by the fire.

The house was very quiet as Patrick settled himself with a pillow at his back and a book on his knees. However tired he might be, he couldn't sleep until he had read a few pages.

Shane gazed out of the window. He never grew weary of the Liffey, especially at night, when the bridges, the lights, the quay walls, and the tall buildings were reflected in the water with the stars and the moon as though another city lay below. In the daytime the reflections were pictures moving in the current but without reality of their own.

Patrick turned a page.

'I'd like to go up to Christ Church another night!' murmured Shane.

Patrick looked up from his book.

'Shane! Have you had any wages yet?'

'Doesn't matter!' answered Shane, over his shoulder. 'I can manage! I was never used to money.'

'Of course it matters!' declared Patrick scornfully. 'We're too proud to sell a copied signature or a book that's worth a great deal of money. But we're not too proud to be in debt to shopkeepers and tradesmen, and Mrs Flanagan and you! It's wrong!'

'I've a good home and all the books I can read! I'm happy!' protested Shane.

'You need money in your pocket! I know you want to buy things for your own people. Why wouldn't you?'

Shane pulled out the sixpence left from the shilling Mrs Flanagan had given him.

'Is that all you have?' asked Patrick sharply. 'Why didn't you remind dadda? Never mind! I'll speak to him in the morning.'

'Don't bother!' declared the other boy. 'I can wait!'

Yet he felt regretful when he remembered he hadn't been able to repay the widow's loan.

He was falling asleep when Patrick began to cough. He sat up. There was a thick haze in the room.

'I'd better shut the window!' said Patrick. 'The fog is coming in from the river.'

Shane was before him. He began to pull the window down when he stopped and blinked in astonishment.

'There's no fog!' he said. 'The night's as clear almost as the night we were out.'

Patrick sniffed.

'I can smell smoke! It can't be dad's pipe. Must be the fire, or it might be someone has a bonfire!'

Shane opened the door and a cloud of smoke billowed into the room.

He started back.

For a moment he stood motionless then, grabbing his clothes, rushed out, followed by Patrick.

'I'll get Bridgie!' he said. 'You rouse the others!'

He stumbled up the winding staircase to find Mr O'Clery trying to open Bridgie's door. But it had stuck!

'Go to the phone!' the bookseller told him. 'Dial O! Ask for the Fire Brigade! Give them the address. Quick!'

Shane dashed through the smoke, down the stairs to the

big room. He dared not attempt to pass through to the shop door, for there were flames in the smoke.

Covering his face with his arm, he pressed along by the wall to the kitchen. The door between the rooms was open but the back one was locked. His fingers trembled so that he found it difficult to turn the key.

At last he succeeded, stepped out into the fresh air, and dashed across the yard into the street.

His excitement made his words run into one another but the operator understood.

Then Shane returned to The Four Masters' Bookshop.

The windows were broken and smoke was pouring out to the street.

'All those books!' thought Shane, with a pang, as he ran into the yard.

Mrs Flanagan stood against the wall, her arms held out. Mr and Mrs O'Clery were piling boxes. Above, at the little window under the roof, Bridgie was leaning out, smoke drifting round her, looking very white and frightened. She held Migeen tightly while Mog stood on the narrow window sill, his tail waving, miaowing anxiously.

'I'll climb up to her!' said Shane.

At the same time he was wondering about Patrick. Where had he got to?

'The boxes will never be high enough!' exclaimed the bookseller. 'We must have a ladder!'

His wife didn't speak. She stood on tiptoe to push a box on the pile already there and, when it tumbled down, just picked it up again and tried to make it firm.

'Let me try!' said Shane.

He scrambled to the top of the boxes and, as they were giving way, sprang upwards. His fingers caught on a projecting stone. He could see Bridgie's eyes fixed on him as he kicked about, feeling for support. But his boots slipped on the thick layers of whitewash and, suddenly, he fell, knocking against the boxes and landing in a heap on the cobbles.

His hands and knees were scraped, a violent pain stabbed his hip, then a black fog descended on him and he lay only half-conscious.

As Shane fell, Patrick's head poked out over the gutter. He had climbed to the roof from the window of his own room, by the big pipe, and thought he would be able to pull Bridgie up beside him. Then the firemen would come with the escape and take them down.

'Get out on the window sill and reach up your hands!' he told his sister.

Bridgie looked up and shook her head.

Even as he spoke, Patrick knew he would never be able to pull her up. Besides, she was too frightened to move and heights made her dizzy. When she looked down at her father and mother their faces were blurred and strange.

'Jump, love! Jump!' urged Mrs Flanagan.

'Try, Bridgie!' urged her mother.

A garda had brought a step-ladder and two men, who had wandered up from the river, were helping him to steady it on the boxes.

'Fetch a blanket!' shouted someone in the crowd at the gate. 'Let's hold it up and the chisellers can drop into it!'

A cloud of smoke swirled round Bridgie. They heard her cry out but now she was almost invisible.

'Out of me way!' said a very determined voice. 'Will no one save that child?'

A tall thin young man, with a shock of red hair, thrust his way into the yard. He pushed Shane with his foot.

'Get up, lad!' he ordered. 'There's work to do!'

Shane opened his eyes and scrambled shakily to his feet.

'Uncle Tim!' he stammered in bewilderment.

'The same! Up here beside me!'

The red-headed man pushed at the boxes, jamming them tight. He mounted them and Shane followed. Then he stooped.

'On me shoulder!' he said.

Shane obeyed.

'Little girl!' said Uncle Tim, speaking very gently. 'Get out on the window sill at once, drop down and Shane will catch you. I'm holding him, so you'll be quite safe. Do as ye're told now!'

Through the smoke Bridgie climbed out on the window sill. Her night-gown was scorched and rumpled. Tears poured down her cheeks, though she made no sound.

'Turn round!' said Uncle Tim. 'Kneel down! Hold on to the sill! Drop yer legs down! Now let go! There's the brave girl!'

Bridgie obeyed and Migeen fell from her grasp. As Shane

caught her, Mr O'Clery grabbed her from his arms. Then Uncle Tim swung Shane to the ground.

'Ye on the roof!' he called. 'Jump! I'll catch ye!'

Patrick couldn't jump from that height but he imitated Bridgie and felt Uncle Tim's strong hands clutching him.

'Puss! Puss!' he called.

With a loud squall of defiance, Mog leaped right down to the yard.

'Here comes the brigade!' the garda told them. 'Isn't it lucky they'll not have the bother of fetching ye young ones down! They'll be able to save what's left of the shop. Stand away there! Stand away!'

People were streaming over the bridges, along the quays. Some were still half-asleep and shivering in the grey dawn.

Now there were more garda. They pressed the people back so that the firemen could do their work. Uncle Tim carried Bridgie out to the street. Patrick and Shane kept as close to him as they could.

Mr O'Clery put his hands over his eyes. He couldn't bear to look on at the burning of his books.

'I'm sorry for this, Mrs O'Clery!' said a very dignified man in a grey tweed suit. 'You shouldn't stay here. You've gone through enough. You must all come round to my house. You remember me? Your husband is one of my clients and we're neighbours!'

Mrs O'Clery looked puzzled and then nodded.

'Of course, you're Michael Deasy, the solicitor. I'm very confused! I don't know what to do!'

'Come with me! That child's had a bad shock! She should be in bed. Let me carry her, Mrs O'Clery!'

Bridgie clung to Tim Madden. He grinned proudly and put Migeen into her hand. Mog rubbed against his leg.

'I'll carry her round!' said Uncle Tim. 'A sup of hot milk, a lie down, and she'll be giving orders before we know where we are! Lead on, mister! After you, má'am! The sooner we're away the better! Follow on, Shane!'

They went in a procession to the grand house, up the steps on the quay near the Four Courts. A gleaming door swung back to let them enter a wide hall, with the smell of the morning's polish hanging on the air.

Shane kept close to his uncle, touching his tattered coat to make sure he was really there. He had forgotten his dream of Tim Madden arriving in a motor, grandly dressed, carrying a brown leather bag and sweeping his nephew off. This was his real Uncle Tim, brave, good-humoured, untidy.

Patrick looked back. He wanted to be with his mother and Bridgie but he didn't like leaving his father.

'Upstairs!' said Mr Deasy. 'Imelda will take care of her!'

Bridgie opened her eyes. Where were they going? She was in Imelda's house. Up the stairs they went and she was in Imelda's room!

It was like a room in the doll's house Bridgie had once owned, with a little blue bed, blue curtains, and a blue chest of drawers. On top, their backs stiffly against the wall, sat two dolls, staring at her. Imelda stood beside them, staring too!

'Will I leave her here, ma'am?' asked Uncle Tim, putting Bridgie on the bed.

She clutched him and looked round to see where her mother was.

Mrs O'Clery drew the blue eiderdown over Bridgie and stepped back.

'Mrs Deasy says you can stay here with Imelda till we've decided what to do. You won't mind, will you?'

Bridgie shook her head but, as the door closed behind her mother and Shane's uncle, she felt very lonely.

'You can have one of my dolls, the one you like best!' said Imelda, bringing over the two dolls and laying them on the bed.

'I'm sorry I threw your doll into the river!' she murmured, turning very red. 'I kept on meaning to come into your shop to tell you. But now you're here, it doesn't matter.'

Bridgie looked at Migeen and smiled.

'No, it doesn't matter!' she said. 'I won't take your doll! I'm too big for dolls. Besides, I have a puppet now!'

The door opened and Imelda's mother came in, carrying a basin of hot bread and milk, with brown sugar sprinkled on the top.

She was a big handsome woman. Bridgie had often seen her driving along in a luxurious car beside Mr Deasy, while Imelda sat in the back seat. Now Bridgie smiled up at her, liking her friendly eyes and the way she settled down on the bed, making it creak under her weight.

'Eat this up, dear! You'll feel better then!'

'I'm not sick!' Bridgie assured her. 'I was frightened, but when Shane's uncle carried me away from the fire I wasn't frightened any more! Where is he?'

'If it's the tall thin man with red hair, he's downstairs, talking. Your mother is there too and the dark boy. I suppose he's your brother. There's another one – a fair lad.'

'That's Shane!' Bridgie told her. 'Tim's his uncle! Can I get up now?'

'Eat your bread and milk first, dear!' said Mrs Deasy.

Bridgie ate the bread and milk steadily. When she was small she always had hot bread and milk on bath nights. Often she wished she hadn't grown too old for such delights.

Imelda stood at the foot of the bed, watching gravely.

'What will happen to Bridgie?' she asked. 'Now the bookshop is burned down she won't have anywhere to live. What will become of her?'

Bridgie lifted her head proudly.

'You don't need to worry about me, Imelda!' she said. 'I've me mammy and me daddy, and Mrs Flanagan, and Patrick and Shane. They'll look after me!'

'Lie down now and sleep!' Mrs Deasy told her.

'I'm not sleepy!' declared Bridgie. 'I want to know all that's happened. I want to – to ...'

Her head fell sideways and she slept.

20. Uncle Tim's Story

Tim Madden straddled a chair and clasped the back, resting his chin on it. Patrick and Shane sat on the window-seat and looked out on the people streaming along to see the last of the fire. Mrs O'Clery, looking bewildered, leaned on the table. A steaming cup of tea was in front of her and she sipped it slowly.

'I must stop drinking tea!' she said. 'This is my seventh cup!'

'You need it!' Mrs Deasy told her. 'It will help you to face your troubles, though, indeed, my husband whispered to me that you have nothing to worry about.'

'Nothing to worry about!' cried Mrs O'Clery. 'It's true we're all safe. But our books! Everything we possessed is destroyed. We'll hardly be able to have a bookstall!'

Mrs Deasy clapped her hands softly.

'Thank God, you're wrong!' she said. 'Michael told me he made your husband insure the shop and stock when he fixed that last agreement for him. You'll have a new shop!'

Mrs O'Clery smiled but shook her head.

'I'm very thankful. But all our first editions that Eugene loves so much, he wouldn't sell them for any price – they're burning away in the fire.'

Uncle Tim stood up.

'If ye'll excuse me, ma'am, I'd like to have a look at what's going on. There might be something we could do and the poor bookseller needs all the help he can get!'

'Stir yerself, Shane lad! Will ye come, Patrick?'

'Isn't it grand to be out in the fresh air!' exclaimed Tim Madden, as he and the two boys went down the steps. 'A house like that would stifle me! Think of that chap living there and, when he comes out, tucks himself into a car with all the grand fresh air shut away. Thanks be, I'm an honest drover and there's always a road for me to walk on! Are ye glad to see me again, lad?'

Suddenly Patrick darted ahead and left them together.

'I am glad!' replied Shane. 'What happened you, Uncle Tim? I went every evening to meet the bus and you never came. I heard of you in Clonmel. Then I got a lift to Dublin and tracked you to Mrs MacNally's of Stoney Batter. Uncle Tim! Did you go to Liverpool? Where have you been? Did you have wonderful adventures? And how did you find me?'

Tim Madden crossed the road and propped himself against the quay wall. Shane stood beside him. They could see the shop of the Four Masters still standing. The flames were dying down but smoke hung over it in a cloud and drifted from the windows. The firemen were standing there, the hose curling about them like serpents. Behind stood Mr O'Clery and the solicitor, watching the spray rising in the air and falling in a steady shower. Patrick stood with them.

'I had desperate adventures!' declared Uncle Tim. 'Twould take all the evenings of winter to tell them. I'm longing to be back with Maureen and the childer. How was Miser Joe when ye last saw him?'

'Cross!' answered Shane.

Tim Madden glanced sideways at the boy and laughed.

'So ye ran away! What did ye do to the man at all?'

Shane told him.

'And when I looked in the bookshop window, and saw *Gulliver's Travels*, the same book you had bought me in

Cork, I couldn't go any further. And they've been terribly good to me! It's wonderful to be there with all those books and Mr O'Clery is always buying more. But now they're burnt!'

He coughed, trying to hide his feelings.

Tim Madden clapped him on the shoulder.

'Have sense, lad! 'Tis a pity the books are destroyed! But what if anything had happened to the little girl? Then you'd have cause for grief! Come along over and we'll see if we can do a job!'

He swaggered across the road.

'Well, sir!' he said to Mr O'Clery. 'Is it ruination or is there something left in the kitty?'

The two men turned to him.

'So you're Shane's uncle!' said the bookseller. 'We've heard great accounts of you!'

'I saw the way you saved that child! It was grand work!' said Mr Deasy, holding out his hand.

Tim gave it a clasp that made the other wince.

'It was grand!' exclaimed the bookseller. 'How can I ever thank you?'

'Is there anything more I can do?' asked Tim Madden. 'I'm on me way south, so if Shane's not wanted, I'll take him home with me! I expect he's as homesick as I am!'

Shane started. Mr O'Clery looked at him in sudden bewilderment.

Tim Madden stooped, picked up the charred fragment of a book, and, laughing, held it out.

Shane read slowly: '*I, Lemuel Gulliver, have given a faithful history of my travels.*'

The blackened words were distinct but a sudden gust of wind swept the page from the young man's hand. It rose in the air and, like a battered crow, swept across the river in the direction of St Patrick's Cathedral.

'*Gulliver's Travels!*' exclaimed Shane. 'Uncle Tim! It was

you started it – buying me that book in Cork! Do you remember? That's the same book! The one I told you I saw in the window!'

'If that don't beat all!' said Tim, frowning a little. 'I remember, ladeen! I've never forgotten, and never will, how ye nearly ate the book!'

'Who is this?' asked Mr Deasy, as a tall man in a wide-brimmed hat strode up to them. He nodded to Shane with a friendly smile.

'That's the American who bought the Dean Swift letter!' the boy whispered to Mr O'Clery.

'I'd like to speak to the man who owns the shop!' said the stranger. 'I just heard the news of the fire!'

'I'm Eugene O'Clery,' the bookseller told him. 'I own the shop – at least what's left of it!'

They shook hands and the solicitor was introduced.

'I wouldn't trouble you at such a time,' said the American. 'But I wondered if I could be of any help? This boy sold me a letter with the signature of that great man, Dean Swift of Dublin. That was real luck for me and I'm grateful!'

'It was a mistake!' Mr O'Clery told him. 'The signature is only a copy. I'll give you back the money at the first opportunity.'

The American looked gravely from one to the other and shook his head.

'I can't take back the money! I made a bargain! If there was a mistake –'

'There was!' both the bookseller and Shane assured him.

'If that's not real bad luck! Can I keep it as a souvenir? If you still have a copy of that great man's work, let me have that and we'll call it quits. I'm staying on a bit longer! I like Dublin! It grows on a man! Call and see me when you have time. You know where I'm staying. We can have a talk – about books or the signatures of famous men!'

He gave his hat a flourish and walked on.

'I'm glad he didn't want his money back!' said Mr O'Clery. 'I'm afraid it's all burnt!'

'Can you be sure?' asked Shane anxiously.

He ran into the yard.

The garda pushed him back.

'Out into the street, me boyo! You're not wanted here!'

'I work here! I live here!' protested the boy.

'Now! Now!' said the man, laughing.

'Indeed I do! Can't I see if there's something I could save?'

'We had to put Mr O'Clery himself out,' explained the garda. 'You see, me lad, we're afraid the roof may fall in. Step aside now! The men are saving all they can!'

As he spoke two men carried out the desk which held the letters and the money. Another followed with an arm-chair.

'Dadda!' called Patrick. 'Here's the desk!'

The bookseller came running. The solicitor followed at a dignified trot. Tim Madden strolled behind them.

'We're saving all we can!' said one of the firemen. 'There's more than you'd expect.'

The bookseller bent over the desk. Before he could take it into the street, Mrs MacNally came panting up to him. A boy marched behind her trundling a wheelbarrow.

'Put it here, Mr O'Clery!' said the lodging-house keeper. 'Mrs Flanagan came and told me the desprit fix ye're in, and ses I to meself – Tim Madden's sure to bring them back with him, so I set two of the chaps clearing out the shed and we've a big front bedroom ready for yerself and the missus! We'll fix up the chisellers before bedtime. Tis a bit of a step but sure ye've a grand pair of long legs under ye!'

She stood gazing at the scene of desolation with such sympathy that Mr O'Clery had to comfort her.

'These grand fellows,' he waved his hand at the grinning firemen, 'have saved my letters and papers. I'm afraid the books have suffered.'

'Bedad! They're bringing out a good few!' she cried, as two men appeared in the doorway, their arms piled with books. 'Here, Thomas! Bring forward the barrer!'

The barrow was loaded with books. Mr O'Clery took the money and letters from the drawer of the desk and that was put on top with the arm-chair.

'Mrs Flanagan will tell him where to put them,' explained Mrs MacNally, 'and the chaps I've left in charge are as honest as the day. All the same, I'll take meself home. Shane Madden, where's Patrick?'

'There he is!'

Patrick came staggering out, carrying a pile of books, his chin keeping them steady.

'I've put that young lad out twice,' grumbled a fireman. 'The chisellers nowadays have no respect!'

Mrs MacNally rolled her eyes.

'Isn't it grand to see them so helpful! Where's me little friend Bridgie?'

'There she is!' said Shane. 'And Mrs O'Clery too!'

'I couldn't stay any longer!' said the bookseller's wife. 'I was worried!'

'Listen, ma'am!' said Mrs MacNally. 'Tomas will be back wid the barrer as soon as he's able! He's taken books, a desk, an arm-chair, and he'll go backwards and forwards for ye till he drops! There's a room ready and waiting and Mrs Flanagan's in charge. I'm on me way now to see to the dinner!'

Mr Deasy smiled.

'You'd all be very welcome at my home,' he said. 'But you might feel freer at Mrs MacNally's. Now I have to take my little daughter to school. Then I must attend to my office. But as soon as I can manage it I'll call on you, Mr O'Clery.'

Mr O'Clery nodded.

'Here's Bridgie!' he said.

She was dressed in one of Imelda's frocks. It was too big and reached to her ankles. Under her arm she had Migeen, and Mog trotted beside her. Imelda, looking very puzzled, followed slowly.

'Suppose I take the ladies to Mrs MacNally's?' suggested Mr Deasy.

'Am I a lady?' asked Bridgie anxiously.

She wanted to see what had happened to her home and the bookshop, but more than all she longed to ride with Imelda in her father's grand car.

'You are a lady!' declared Mr Deasy, with such a low bow Bridgie grew hot all over.

'Maybe I should go and arrange our things at the other end!' said Mrs O'Clery.

She didn't want to leave her husband alone with the burnt-out shop but she knew someone should be at Mrs MacNally's to help Mrs Flanagan.

'If it's not troubling you too much, Mr Deasy,' she said.

'The car is across the road,' he told her, bowing again.

'Hasn't he the lovely manners! Ye should be very proud of yer da, Miss Imelda!' exclaimed Mrs MacNally.

Imelda was so delighted she flushed and her eyes sparkled.

'She is really lovely!' thought Bridgie, who hadn't been too pleased with Imelda since she had thrown Migeen into the Liffey.

But look how well it had turned out! Here was the rag doll, now a clever puppet, able to do all manner of tricks – with a bit of encouragement!

Mrs O'Clery stepped into the car first, with the solicitor holding the door open for her. Bridgie and Mrs MacNally sat with her. Imelda was in front with her father.

It was grand to drive along the quay, with buses and lorries and other motors all around them. Up they sped to Stoney Batter. Bridgie sat very straight and showed Migeen the sights. Mog was curled up as tightly as he could manage on Mrs O'Clery's lap. He didn't care for big fires – such an upset!

Imelda's eyes grew very big when she saw where the passengers were going. But she waved and smiled as her father turned the car.

She saw Mrs Flanagan, the old coat flapping about her, holding out her arms as Bridgie rushed to her, followed by Mog, whiskers bristling, tail erect. They passed out of sight into Mrs MacNally's. The door closed and the car sped citywards.

21. Home for Christmas

It was crowded at Mrs MacNally's, for she couldn't and wouldn't turn out her regular drover lodgers. But they were obliging people and agreed to share rooms and beds, so that the O'Clerys could stay until they had a home again. In the mornings Shane went with Tim to the Cattle Market. The rest of the time he helped Mr O'Clery.

'I'd love to go down to Cork and me pockets filled with money!' declared Tim.

'Will Uncle Joseph want us back?' asked the boy.

He was worried. He longed to go to the farm loaded with presents, to watch Aunt Maureen and Maggie, little Babs and the boys untie the string and fold back the brown paper. Yet how could he leave Dublin? He'd be miserable if he didn't see the O'Clerys again. They'd been so good to him and he loved the shop!

Only now – there wasn't a shop!

But there would be!

Tim tossed a penny into the air.

'Now we'll see if Joseph will welcome us. If the hen turns up, he'll cheer when he sees us. If it's the harp, he runs us!'

The penny fell on the floor – harp side up!

Tim chuckled.

'I'm afeard tis the truth! If it had been the hen I wouldn't have believed it. Brother-in-law Joseph doesn't want me! But

Maureen does! And the young ones will go mad when they see us poking in our heads!'

He glanced at Shane's serious face.

'Ye don't want to go to the farm – is that it? I understand. Ye've made a real home here! Only I'm sorry for Maureen!'

'I do want to go back!' protested Shane. 'I want to see them all. Only I couldn't bear never to live with the O'Clerys and not to work in the shop again. I want to stay here and I want to go with you to the farm. I don't know what to do!'

Tim nodded.

'Ye're like meself!' he said slowly. 'I always want to go! I always want to stay! Don't worry! We'll find a way!'

Mrs Flanagan and the children cleaned the house from top to bottom. Then they started decorating. As Christmas drew near, all the drovers went to their own homes, except two who had nowhere else to go. They chopped logs until there was a great pile outside the kitchen window.

It was only a week to Christmas when Tim came in before dinner, loaded with parcels.

'D'ye know what's happened?' he cried excitedly.

Shane had been helping Mr O'Clery sort out the heaps of half-soaked, half-burned books still lying at the back of the shop. He was washing his face and hands under the tap in Mrs MacNally's kitchen. He looked round through a lather of soap-suds and shook his head.

'Mr O'Clery gave me ten pounds for saving his young one!' said Tim. 'Saving! That's what he called it! He's had some of his insurance money and he insisted on me taking it. That solicitor chap was there and he told me I should. So I'm made up! Could ye do wid a pound note, young Shane?'

The boy shook his head.

'Mr O'Clery's giving me ten shillings a week and I get me keep. Thank you all the same! I've bought me presents and there's a surprise for everyone!'

'Good lad!' said Uncle Tim. 'What about a farewell jaunt

through the city? I'd like to tell Maureen what Dublin looks like at Christmas. She was always a great one for the lights and the crowds!'

Bridgie and Patrick had seen Santa Claus ride along O'Connell Street on a sleigh drawn by four white horses but, after tea, they were quite willing to set off again. They felt proud to show Uncle Tim the splendours of the city.

'We must do it all in order!' declared Patrick. 'We don't want Tim Madden to miss anything!'

'Dublin's such a big place!' Shane told his uncle.

They went along Henry Street and it was hard to believe that this fairyland of lights and colour was the same street they used as a short cut on their way to the Pro-Cathedral every Sunday morning.

Chains of lights hung from one side to the other. Over a big furniture shop the silver sails of a windmill turned slowly. An unseen player tossed a golden ball into the darkness. When it disappeared he flung another and another, until Bridgie stood staring up into the sky wondering where they had flown. Shane and Tim held her hands, drawing her along with them until they came to the tall pillar where Nelson stands gazing over the city.

Here the tree sparkled with coloured lights which vanished, then sparkled into light again, unceasingly. Along the front of the high grey buildings hung huge lanterns – pink, green, blue, yellow, red – and above them Christmas trees were perched on the wide window sills.

Bridgie and Patrick were used to the beauty of Dublin at night time but to Shane it was still strange and lovely as a fairy city.

They crossed O'Connell Bridge and stood for a moment against the parapet looking up towards the dome of the Four Courts. Along there was the ruined shop and they wondered how soon it would rise again. Then the crowd swept them to the south side of the river.

The current was flowing seaward but the wind blew against it and the dark surface of the water tossed up in white, foaming crests. They went through the narrow alleys and came out upon the road leading up to Dublin Castle. Crossing over, once again they came to a street of many lights.

The shop windows were still and quiet. The crowds passing before them were quiet too. Buses rumbled by and, high against the great buildings, moving pictures in lights kept people craning upwards. At the end of the street a giant Christmas tree raised gleaming branches.

'I do wish Maggie and Babs and the boys could see all this!' said Tim regretfully. 'I'd like them to know a bit of the grandeur of Christmas! Mebbe I could take them into Cork!'

They listened to the carol singers and, when Bridgie was tired, turned homeward. They left the glittering crowded streets behind and trudged along the quays, lit only by the street lamps.

By the time they reached the Metal Bridge, Bridgie was dragging her feet and blinking sleepily.

'Up on me shoulder!' said Uncle Tim. 'I don't know what ye're going to do when yer riding horse is down in County Cork!'

So she rode in triumph until they came to the shop, which now had a high fence round it.

Mr O'Clery was standing there, smoking. He waved his pipe at them.

'If I could have a word with young Shane?' he said.

'I'll see the chisellers safe home,' Tim told him.

They went on to Stoney Batter while Shane and the bookseller stood looking at the dark flowing river.

Slowly they followed the others.

'I know you won't go back with your uncle because you don't like to leave us in a fix,' said the bookseller suddenly. 'Yet we won't be able to open the shop for a while. There's no reason why you shouldn't go to your people for a holiday and return after Christmas.'

Shane stood gazing at the lighted bridges and the high dark buildings beyond the river. He bit his lip – to go back, to sit beside Aunt Maureen and tell her all that had happened, to watch Maggie's eyes growing big with wonder, to have the boys think him a hero and a traveller, to hand round the presents he had bought! He could hardly believe it!

'You mean I can go home with Uncle Tim and then come back to the shop?' stammered the boy.

Mr O'Clery laughed.

'That's what I mean! Are you happy with us, Shane?'

Shane nodded.

'I am, Mr O'Clery! Only I was feeling I'd like to see me aunt and me cousins. Aunt Maureen was real good to me and Maggie's a great little girl. She's as good as Bridgie!'

'When we're back in our own home you can bring her up for a holiday!' the bookseller told him. 'Then your

Uncle Tim will be coming to Dublin often, now you're here!'

'Mr O'Clery! When we have the new shop would you put *Gulliver's Travels* in the window again?'

Mr O'Clery sighed.

'I'll have to get a new copy. Both the old ones are destroyed!'

'That doesn't matter!' said Shane. 'Jonathan Swift would like to have his book there!'

The bookseller looked down at the boy walking beside him, then across the Liffey to where Christ Church and St Patrick's rose into the clear frosty air.

'He would! I'd like to think he'd cross the river sometimes and see his book in my shop.'

As they climbed the road leading up to the Cattle Market, they saw Tim on the steps of Mrs MacNally's house. He beckoned and Shane started running.

'I'm on me way!' shouted Tim. 'I've the offer of a lift on a lorry!'

Patrick and Bridgie were standing behind him, looking very mournful.

'Listen, lad!' said Tim. 'Come with me! There's Maureen and the young ones! Run up! Fetch yer duds and we'll be off wid ourselves!'

'I will! And Mr O'Clery says I can come back after Christmas!' Shane told his uncle. 'I'll get me things!'

'They're here!'

Mrs MacNally came down the hall with Shane's bundle.

'I knew you'd never let the uncle go alone!' she said. 'Here's the lorry! Good luck now! This is a bite for the journey!'

She gave Shane a big brown-paper parcel.

A lorry, loaded with bulging sacks and crates, drew up at the kerb. Tim swung his bundle in among them.

'On board, lad!' he said, pushing Shane up.

Suddenly the doorway was crowded.

'Safe home!' called Bridgie and Patrick.

'Don't forget to come back!' cried Mr O'Clery.

'Happy Christmas!' shouted Shane and Uncle Tim.

'Hold tight!' roared the driver.

Away went the lorry. Tim pushed the boy into a nest among the crates and drew their bundles after them.

'Settle down!' he said. 'Tis a long journey!'

Shane blinked.

Shops and houses fell away behind them. They were part of the stream of lighted cars and lorries.

The house on Stoney Batter, the O'Clerys, Mrs Flanagan, Mrs MacNally – all the friends Shane had made, were no longer there. He was alone with Uncle Tim!

'Pull the sacks over ye, me boyo! Are ye warm? Isn't it grand to be on the road again!'

'I'm glad I'll be seeing Aunt Maureen and Maggie!' said Shane.

'We'll take the whole bang shoot of them into Cork and buy them everything they take a fancy to! We'll bring Joseph! This will be a Christmas to remember!'

'We will come back to Dublin, won't we, Uncle Tim?'

'We will, lad! We will! Doesn't the whole world come back to Dublin?'

Also by Patricia Lynch

KNIGHTS OF GOD

Here, in a beautifully told mixture of history and legend, are the stories of some of Ireland's greatest saints, told by one of Ireland's best story-tellers.

You can learn of the slavery of St Patrick, the patron saint of Ireland, of his adventurous escape, and his return to convert the Irish; of St Brendan and his strange voyages to magical, mysterious islands; of St Brigid and St Kevin and their wonderful friendships with animals, and of Lawrence O'Toole, the last in the great procession of Irish saints, who fought so hard to save Ireland from invasion by the Norman English.

KING OF THE TINKERS

There was once a boy, the son of a fiddler, who lived with his widowed mother in a cabin in Ireland; she earned their living by selling socks and mufflers at the fair, and excellent eggs from their ten magic hens.

Then one night Miheal heard a troop of tinkers going by; in the morning one of the hens was missing. And so it went on: however well Miheal kept watch, one by one the tinkers spirited the birds away, until Miheal and his mother were in a very sad way.

So of course Miheal set off to rescue the precious hens, get his father's stolen fiddle back again and settle accounts with Yellow Handkerchief, the cleverest thief in the whole wide world.

If you have enjoyed this book and would like to know about others which we publish, why not join the Puffin Club? You will receive the club magazine, *Puffin Post*, four times a year and a smart badge and membership book. You will also be able to enter all the competitions. For details send a stamped addressed envelope to:

The Puffin Club, Dept. A
Penguin Books Limited
Bath Road,
Harmondsworth
Middlesex